Bello:

hidden talent rediscovered

Bello is a digital only imprint of Pan Macmillan,
established to breathe new life into previously published,
classic books.

At Bello we believe in the timeless power of the imagination,
of good story, narrative and entertainment and we want to use
digital technology to ensure that many more readers
can enjoy these books into the future.

We publish in ebook and Print on Demand formats
to bring these wonderful books to new audiences.

About Bello:

www.panmacmillan.com/bello

*Sign up to our newsletter to hear about
new releases, events and competitions:*

www.panmacmillan.com/bellonews

Jo Bannister

Jo Bannister lives in Northern Ireland, where she worked as a journalist and editor on local newspapers. Since giving up the day job, her books have been shortlisted for a number of awards. Most of her spare time is spent with her horse and dog, or clambering over archaeological sites. She is currently working on a new series of psychological crime/thrillers.

Jo Bannister

A CACTUS GARDEN

BELL

First published in 1983 by Hale

This edition published 2012 by Bello
an imprint of Pan Macmillan, a division of Macmillan Publishers Limited
Pan Macmillan, 20 New Wharf Road, London N1 9RR
Basingstoke and Oxford
Associated companies throughout the world

www.panmacmillan.com/imprints/bello

ISBN 978-1-4472-3636-8 EPUB
ISBN 978-1-4472-3635-1 POD

Copyright © Jo Bannister, 1983

The right of Jo Bannister to be identified as the
author of this work has been asserted in accordance
with the Copyright, Designs and Patents Act 1988.

A CIP catalogue record for this book is available from the British Library.

Printed and bound by CPI Group (UK) Ltd, Croydon, CR0 4YY

Visit **www.panmacmillan.com** to read more about all our books
and to buy them. You will also find features, author interviews and
news of any author events, and you can sign up for e-newsletters
so that you're always first to hear about our new releases.

Strong Enchantments

Chapter One

Alone in the jewelled darkness of her cell, high under the blind cone of the Hive, enthroned in unobserved majesty, the lady Amalthea sat and brooded.

A black cloak, gem-starred, shrouded her, even to her head, and her face was lost in the deep shade of its enveloping hood. Only a long narrow hand displayed on the leather arm of the black throne, almost but never quite still, twitching in fractional reflection of the mighty thoughts churning in her mind, the scant movement sending ruby and emerald glints up the secret walls from her heavy jewelled rings, betrayed the shadowy form as something living and aware. The long pale fingers ended in long black claws, ticking restlessly on the black hide.

Within the hood, within the shrouded head, Amalthea's brain pounded with fifteen years' frustration. Before that had been ages in the wilderness, so that her coming to Mithras had seemed a triumph. She had conquered utterly, none had stood against her – for the wilderness had made her strong and ruthless, and desperate, and also the natives were not warriors – and the richness of the taken place had dazzled and delighted her. While the Drones laboured to roll back the jungle and dig foundations for the great Hive, she herself had plucked from the rent earth the raw gems that now bore down her fingers. She wore them always. They stated louder than words, This world is mine.

But the concept of possession, of having and holding, was not unique to the people of the Hive. The conquered world exacted a cruel vengeance, subtle as smoke, bitter as a Judas kiss. If it was true that Amalthea brought little mercy to Mithras, it was equally so that none existed there before. All but hidden in the deep folds of the hood, amethyst eyes kindled darkly at the memory of the disaster, devastatingly apposite, humiliatingly complete, which had broken over the Hive in the very spring of its people's flowering. Since then Amalthea's task had been to hold together her stunned clan, to give them a unity in isolation and a purpose where there was no future, and to direct their despair outward where it might armour the Hive and not, as was the great danger, inward to consume its children. She had been their saviour – guide, general, queen and god. Without her ruthless determined leadership they could not have survived. Now, after fifteen years, their faith in her would be vindicated. Amalthea could smell salvation.

She was no longer alone. A man stood in the open door, back-lit by the glow from the hall, waiting silently to be recognised. Amalthea turned the black window of her hood slowly towards him. "Michal."

The man said, in a young man's voice, "Lady, the people from the ship are arrived." His voice was brittle with repressed excitement.

Amalthea rose, the black shroud falling softly, weightlessly, from her. Michal averted his eyes reverently. In the dim high room she shone like a column of moonlight, her shift of silver mail rippling from throat to ankle. Short silver hair capped her narrow sculpted skull; eyes like black grapes smouldered in her pointed face. Her white arms were bare, and silver bangles clustered above her left elbow. Her purple eyes and her dark lips and the two jewels on her long hand were the only colour about her. She was small and all her youth was fled, but she was beautiful and awesome, and her people both adored and feared her greatly. They called her Morningstar.

Amalthea moved to the open doorway. The young man fell back to let her pass. She paused beside him. "The ship?"

"As you instructed, lady."

Satisfaction ghosted across Amalthea's face and her pointed chin rose. Her voice was light with pleasure. "Why then, Michal," she said, "I am an empress again." She passed into the golden hall.

Sharvarim-besh, who had been patiently waiting for the messenger to return, saw Amalthea make her entrance on the gallery above the long hall, a shaft of moongleam in the sun temple, and caught her breath in admiration. Paul, who resented waiting for anybody and was studiously looking the other way when the lady of Mithras appeared, avoided the impact of the moment and did not turn round until Shah nudged him and whispered, "Look."

Paul turned without haste, to find himself held like a moth on a pinboard in a scrutiny whose fierce hostility he could fathom the length of the glowing chamber. "Ah, there you are," he said pointedly.

Shah's heart thumped painfully in her breast; keyed up tighter than a lute-string, she anticipated catastrophe with every beat. This was where the greatest danger lay – more than in battle, perhaps even more than in defeat. Paul had wanted to leave her on "Gyr", but Shah refused; he asked for three good reasons, she provided them. She had not seen so many worlds that she was incurious about Mithras; left alone on "Gyr" while Paul negotiated his contract with the alien queen she would be butchered by anxiety; and if the worst happened she would be more capable of fending for herself on the surface than on a ship where the only instrumentation she understood was the clock.

So he acquiesced and took her to meet Amalthea, landing the shuttle on the broad swathe of bare earth which girdled the forest clearing whose hub was the swollen, gravid shape of the great Hive. Before the burners were out a motley crew of Mithraians had gathered and were anointing the little craft with oil. Paul locked it up and left them to it. Whether the ritual had religious or practical significance, whether it was ordained or just their own small tribute, he had no idea, but he was confident that nothing they could do to the outside of the shuttle would affect its ability to fly.

He had not exaggerated the risk inherent in initial meetings between mercenaries and potential employers. Each had much to lose and much to gain by cheating. In the essence of the business, the employer had something worth protecting and money to pay for its protection but not the technology to do the job himself: an unscrupulous mercenary could set his cap at the valuables happy in the knowledge that their owner had not the strength to oppose him. The distinction between mercenary and privateer grew often woolly at the edges.

No less common was the reciprocal situation, when an employer decided that rather than pay to have his war fought he should seize the mercenary's equipment, dispose of the mercenary, fight the war and keep all the spoils himself. Not infrequently some chieftain in whom the spirit of free enterprise burnt particularly strongly would begin with the latter manoevre and proceed by way of the former. Paul considered that cowboys like that got professionals like him a bad name. Shah wondered privately how you could slander a man who killed other men for money.

There was another reason she wanted to be there when Paul met Amalthea. The mercenary was sharp and swift-witted, cunning and astute and familiar with all the sneakier devices, but if mischief were afoot Shah would know before he would. Shah could read minds.

Amalthea came down the stair from the gallery, a shimmering silver vision calculated to steal breath from the cynical and impress the worldly-wise. She gave, as she intended to give, an overwhelming first impression of female power – intellectual and carnal, sacred and profane. A hard bright sovereignty which democracy could not scratch surrounded her and spoke to people too far distant to discern her face. She walked as women walk, but the watchers detected in her liquid unforced movements the same enormity, the same latent explosiveness, as marks natural phenomena like tidal waves and lava flows and other irresistible consumptions. With her purple eyes and her taut, purposeful body brimming with sensual energy, like a whirlwind with the lid on, she had been compared with cruel creatures of the night. But in truth Amalthea was the personification of night itself, great and cold and incapable of being hindered, less cruel than unyielding, less savage than implacable. She was a woman halfway to becoming an element.

She advanced down the long hall like a sweeping twilight, without haste and without a pause. The travellers made no move towards her: Shah because she had no idea of the protocol of these occasions and Paul because he never met anyone halfway.

The young man Michal watchful at her heels as a hound, Amalthea – neither her composure nor the metre of her stride disturbed by apprehension – walked towards Paul until she was within handstrike of him. Then she stopped and stared him in the eye and said silkily, "If you have any thought of cheating me, Paul, forget it now."

Shah blinked. She had expected ceremony, careful elaborate fencing to establish positions and strengths, perhaps a subtle trial of wills. She had not expected a woman of uncertain but advanced years, so diminutive she looked small even beside Paul, who would march up to the mercenary and fix him with her feline gaze and spell out the ground rules, while all the time his gunship circled over her head.

Paul too was impressed, though he would have died rather than admit it. He returned her gaze with frank interest. His eyes were as strange as hers, with dark irises flecked with gold. "Lady," he said, "I think you and I feel the same way about business, so I'll be honest with you. I have no intention of cheating you. If we can agree terms I will prosecute this war for you, and win it, and take my money and leave. If you try to seize my ship, or withhold my fee, or sell me to your enemies as the price of peace, or attempt any of the other friendly deceits that give rise to such complications in this line of work, I will blow your little conical city off the face of this globe."

Amalthea's red lip curled. "You talk boldly for a man a hundred miles below his power-base and well inside mine."

"Automation is a prime feature of a battle-cruiser that can be flown in combat by one man. 'Gyr' passes overhead every eighty-five minutes. When she does so I signal her. When I signal her, she doesn't open fire."

The lady of Mithras eyed him warily, more inclined to believe him than not, the implications of acceptance chattering up in her brain like a computer display. "How do you signal?"

Paul grinned, a wolfish grin that split his narrow weathered face with a sudden ferocity that still made Shah startle. "If I were foolish enough to tell you that, you wouldn't want to hire me."

Amalthea also smiled. Her smile had a quality like cracking ice. "If you were foolish enough to tell me that," she purred, "I would not have to hire you."

Shah, wondering how a contract could be executed against a backdrop of deep mutual distrust, failing to appreciate that mutuality provided a working substitute for stability, found herself the focus of imperious eyes the colour of grape-bloom. Amalthea said nothing: she looked from Shah to Paul and raised one fine upswept brow clear of her amethyst lid. Shah could not be sure if her lids were stained or their skin so palely translucent that the colour of her eyes bled through.

Paul caught the look and interpreted it. "Sharvarim-besh. My associate."

Shah had wondered how he would introduce her. Associate. Well, that was non-committal enough even for him.

Patently Amalthea would have preferred to negotiate on a one-to-one basis. Equally obviously, if lieutenants he had to bring, she would have preferred them male. Her sex gave her an advantage that she was loathe to see devalued by inflation. "If your ship can be flown in combat by one man," she said coldly, "what does she do?"

Shah smiled her sweetest smile. Her long coltish body and dramatically dark colouring did not sit with sweetness but she did her best. "Oh, make the beds, wash the pots, tell him who to work for – little things like that."

Paul chuckled, rather enjoying the sensation of being quarrelled over, and did not contradict. Amalthea flicked them the briefest of smiles, and walked past them and through the door behind. "Accommodation has been prepared. Michal will conduct you there. We will talk again later."

"We'll look forward to that," Paul assured her departing back.

Following the steward along blind corbelled passages he remarked to Shah, "As an interplanetary diplomat you may well be in my class. Your first professional engagement, your first alien head of state, your first words – and you make an enemy."

Left alone to explore their apartment, Shah looked for clues to the nature of the Hive people and Paul looked for listening devices. The apartment consisted of seven interlocking hexagonal cells: a living-room surrounded by – working clockwise – the entrance lobby, dining-room, kitchen, bedroom, bathroom and second bedroom. The rooms were furnished with that opulent simplicity typical of sophisticated societies, with the larger items in plastics and the details in precious metals.

Paul returned from the lobby where he had been running his fingers around the door-frame. "Well, if there's a bug it's built-in and I can't do anything about it."

Shah returned from the kitchen. "These people cook in the weirdest way!"

"Microwaves."

"Everything's made of pot. There aren't any pans."

"You can't use metal with microwaves."

"But *everything's* made of pot. I can't find anything in ordinary metal – just silver and gold. The cutlery's all silver, even the tin-opener and the corkscrew."

"That is odd," admitted Paul. He prowled round, touching things – hefting the table-lamps, prodding the taps; he pulled the linen off one of the beds to see how it was constructed. "There's no hard metal here," he said finally. "Copper in the lamps and in the oven, tin cans in the cupboard, gold where hardness isn't at a premium, silver where it is. I think silver is the hardest metal they have."

"What does that mean – no iron ore?"

"Possibly. But there are other hard metals, and they haven't used any of them. They have tin and copper but no bronze. They use silver instead of steel and gold instead of aluminium. They have a base metal famine." He went on prowling. "That could be because there's no suitable ore available; or it could be that something happens to hard metals here. That might explain the guard of honour who met us with oil-cans when we landed. Do you want to know what I think?"

"You think that Mithras has a peculiarly corrosive atmosphere that destroys all the harder metals, and that is why the Hive – despite an advanced theoretical technology – is unable to get into space and thus defend itself against those who can."

Paul glared at her. "I've told you to stay out of my head," he said in his teeth.

"You flatter yourself," retorted Shah. "Your head isn't the only place around here that deductions can be made."

"You thought that?"

"I thought that."

"I'm glad," said Paul after a moment, slumping into the bosom of a great semi-circular settee, one of a pair that bracketed the living-room. "I should hate to be responsible for anything that sloppy."

Shah snorted with unladylike derision.

"Theoretical technology doesn't take you from copper smelting to microwaves. If you can't make bronze you settle for taking the kinks out of the arrowheads and putting them back in the fish-hooks after every hunt. You don't set about designing sophisticated substitutes for simple non-availables. In short, you don't build a computer because the fur on your fingers makes you clumsy with an abacus."

"Paul – what do you think?" Though he eyed her suspiciously Shah maintained a straight face, folding her strong hands in her lap demurely as she took the opposite settee.

"I think they're aliens here themselves. This isn't their planet: they evolved somewhere else, somewhere that normal metallurgy was possible so that their development to the space exploration stage was unhindered. Perhaps they came here precisely because of the copious deposits of precious metals. But the vessel which brought them down onto the surface was affected. They couldn't leave. Depending on when all this was, the Hive people were on that ship or are descended from those who were. They are heirs of a civilisation that could never have evolved on Mithras."

"So now they have gold taps and silver corkscrews, and hire mercenaries to fight their battles for them," mused Shah. "Are they content?"

"I should think so," Paul supposed idly. "If they didn't want to stay they could have called up a liner instead of a battle-cruiser and left the place to the pirates."

"Perhaps that's why they don't use wood," volunteered Shah. "There's none of that either, despite ninety per cent of the land masses of Mithras being covered with forests. Perhaps where these people came from there were no trees. Perhaps they're actually frightened of trees, and that's why there are no windows in the Hive. Perhaps –"

"Perhaps it's time you stopped speculating on matters you know nothing about and gave me the benefit of that small talent you do possess."

Laughter sparkled in Shah's great almond-shaped eyes, and she leaned forward conspiratorially. "You know, if these walls do have ears and if Amalthea is listening, she'll take quite the wrong inference from that!"

Paul grinned. "Speaking of which, I see that cohabitation is discouraged. Two bedrooms, and two very definitely single beds. Even the couches are curved!"

"I think the lady is a prude."

Paul leaned back, looking at her, heavy lids drooping over his eyes. Another man might have seemed sleepy: this one had the hooded, predatory look of a leopard mentally tucking in its napkin. "What else do you think of the lady?"

"You mean, can we trust her? I don't know, Paul, it's too early. That wasn't much of a meeting. I never really got into her at all. She was – elated; maybe more than was reasonable. Despite what she said, she isn't afraid of being cheated. She isn't afraid of you." Shah frowned, the beginnings of concern in the backs of her eyes. "I'm not sure, in all the circumstances, she should be that confident."

Paul smiled lazily. "She just has more faith in me than you have. I find that perceptive rather than suspicious. Anything more?"

"No – only that she doesn't like me, and I imagine even you –" Shah stopped abruptly, pain twisting up her face. "Oh Paul, I'm sorry, I didn't mean –"

"Will you stop being so sensitive on my behalf?" he said gruffly.

"You're right, it didn't take a telepath to see that, which is lucky enough because I'm not a telepath any longer. I know it, you know it: there's nothing to walk shy of. Don't bleed for me, Shah. If I'm hurt I can do it for myself, but that particular wound is healing nicely – it doesn't need to be handled through a glove-box."

"I know. I'm sorry." She leaned forward and took his hand in both of hers. In her smile was the deep friendship that was his only valued possession which he did not count his by right, hard-earned by blood, sweat, toil and – though usually other people's – tears. He did not know why Shah stayed with him. Most of the time he did not wonder, but when he did the fact that he could find no logical explanation of her loyalty, and therefore no explicit reason for its enduring, was a cold spot in his heart that all his conditioning prevented him from recognising as fear.

"But Paul, you and I are closer than you care to admit. When you are hurt I cannot but feel it; if I cry out when you keep silent it is because I am less strong than you. I know you'd be happier if I too could be calm and pragmatic and unemotional, but I'm not made that way; and you are dear to me."

Paul stared into her face intently for a long minute. Then he rose, his hand pulling free of hers, and went into the kitchen. Shah straightened up with a sigh, disappointed with herself and with Paul, despairing of progress in her self-appointed task of humanising him. His voice reached her through the open door, muffled – as if he had his head in the strange oven. "Anyway, you're wrong. I don't want you to change. Not now I've gone to all the trouble of getting used to you."

Shah said nothing. She smiled to herself. She looked around the hypocritically Spartan room and thought, We could always push the couches together.

Late into the night – though the passing of the light meant little in the Hive – Amalthea presided over a meeting of the Council.

The Council of Mithras was not a democratic body. It did as Amalthea instructed it. Its function was primarily to relieve the lady of the tedium of disseminating her wishes personally: she told the Council what she wanted and the Councillors worked out how best to satisfy her. That was in matters of routine. In this matter Amalthea was settling all the details herself.

The Council met in a dark hexagonal chamber in the secret heart of the Hive. Like the lady's own cell, its surfaces were faced with a matt black that stole perspective and any sense of time or place. Unlike Amalthea's room, the blackness was unrelieved by the fire of jewels or the glint of gold. The chamber's only feature was its great table, echoing the shape of the room, hollow-hearted. The table and the chairs drawn up two to a side were made of clear perspex. Framed by the table was a raised dais from which, suitably elevated above her Council, Amalthea ruled Mithras from a revolving chair. The fact that the Council numbered thirteen had no particular significance for the Mithraians, but nor was it wildly inappropriate.

Amalthea was speaking. She sprawled gracefully in her elegant, eminent chair, an idly sculling slipper turning her slowly round the faces of her Councillors, and her voice was also slow, but there was nothing idle or inconsequential in either her words or her delivery.

"These people are to feel at home here. They are to be treated with friendship and kindness, to be facilitated and humoured, to be put at their ease. And if anyone, by word or deed, well-meant or unintentional, gives rise to the least suspicion on their part regarding my motives, I will give him to the planet on the same day that I give it them."

Chapter Two

There was a tap at the door. Shah answered it and found the young man Michal in the corridor, shifting nervously from one foot to the other. "Hello."

"The lady Amalthea's compliments, and she wondered – I wondered – we thought your ladyship might like to see something of the Hive." He finished on a note of relief, although his message could not have been simpler or more cordially received. He seemed very young, although he was probably Shah's age.

"Come in. I'll consult the oracle."

Shyly he followed her into the lobby. The living-room door was open; so was the door opposite, through which he could see the foot of a bed draped with softly flowing female things. Shah saw his look and reflected ruefully that she had not been there twenty-four hours and already the place was a dump. She shrugged. "I'm afraid I told your lady a lie. I don't even make the beds – not with any regularity. Paul?"

She did not see that Michal's eyes on her scattered clothes were burning, or that he turned away with heat in his cheeks and blinked rapidly several times and bit his lip. "Paul, I'm being offered a guided tour."

Paul was in the bathroom, shaving. Like many small dark men he had a strong beard, and he heartily grudged the time he wasted daily keeping it at bay, yet he would neither let it grow nor use one of the aerosol growth inhibitors which he considered in some ways effeminate. He may well have been the last man in the civilised cosmos to scrape hair off his face with a naked blade.

There was a splash of water, and he appeared, drying his face.

"I heard. You'd better go. See all you can: if Amalthea and I can't reach agreement we may not be here long."

"What if she calls another meeting this morning?"

"I'll try to get by without you."

Michal sneaked a look at them together. Their casual intimacy, which seemed to mean nothing to either of them, stabbed him with envy like knives.

"All right, but don't sign anything," cautioned Shah.

"How did I ever manage before I knew you?" wondered Paul, and threw his towel at her head, stumped into the bedroom and slammed the door. It was not the bedroom where the woman's things were laid out. Michal's heart leapt and raced on in a way that he did not understand. He kept his eyes on the floor and hoped fervently that his discomposure was less obvious than the blood thundering in his ears and the sweat breaking in his palms seemed to suggest. Michal was a 24-year-old virgin with the emotional maturity of a pubescent schoolboy.

He looked up quickly, stammering, a hunted look in his face. "What?"

Shah smiled kindly. "I said, I'm ready when you are."

Michal held the door for her, caught her scent as she passed, felt his lurching heart plummet with the knowledge – certain as despair – that she saw him for a fool.

The blueprint for the Great Hive of Mithras could not have sprung from a sane mind. It defied all the conventions of architecture and structural engineering, and trying to discern patterns or principles in its flambuoyantly random alignment gave Shah a sensation like motion-sickness. The Hive was a coil, like a snake in a basket, spiralling slowly up from a broad torus to the domed apex where Amalthea had her quarters. Because of this arrangement none of the floors was quite flat and none of the walls was quite vertical, and the deviations increased not only from level to level but also from the core to the outside wall. Someone with enough time, patience and stamina could climb from basement to apogee without mounting a step merely by following the spiral round, but for those in a hurry there were stairs, in bizarre staggered flights which connected only alternate levels.

The conducted tour began at the top, or as near the top as any save the chosen few were permitted. "The audience chamber," said Michal. It was the long golden hall where they had met Amalthea. On that occasion appreciation had been tempered by her own anxiety, by Paul smouldering watchfully on one side of her and Amalthea sparking on the other. Now she gave it the attention it demanded.

Everything in the hall was golden, and much of it was gold. The floor was tiled in glowing ceramics, intricately patterned. Fabric hangings shot through with metallic thread clad the long walls. Gilt and crystal chandeliers clustered thickly under the coffered ceiling, where black enamel beams framed burning panels of gold leaf. A waist-high dado of beaten gold girdled the room, and gold liveries decked a retinue of alabaster servants watching the doors with sightless gaze.

Shah shook her head in amazement. The audience chamber was a spectacle, crowding the eyes, delivering its message with the delicacy of cudgel-blows: that those who made it and kept it had wealth and power beyond comprehension, and that those summoned to it –however well-placed they might consider themselves in other company – were dross here and had better not forget it. Shah began to understand Michal's habit of dropping his eyes. The golden hall was not specifically to impress the occasional visitor; it was to awe the Hive masses, to remind them of their place. The chamber was brilliant, opulent, gorgeous and glorious and incredibly rich; also crass, over-weening, without subtlety or finesse, its grandeur unimpeached by any style. There was a degeneracy about it, a corruption, a paradoxical poverty of ideals. It was a monument to insensitivity.

Shah wondered what Michal, who worked here without sharing in the status which it represented and defended, thought of the gilt cavern. She sidled carefully into his unguarded mind, but Michal was thinking of something else, and Shah slipped out again quickly with a grin. She turned her back on the glittering waste, winked at the unresponsive statues, and startled Michal beyond measure by linking her arm through his. "Come on, show me where the real people are."

There were no real people; not in the sense that Shah and Michal and Paul and even Amalthea, with her talons and her towering arrogance, were real. There were mannequins, two-dimensional peacocks strutting the walkways and coagulating in idle, languorous groups around the stairs. They ignored Michal and stared at Shah with overt curiosity, covert hostility and, in their secret minds where only a telepath could pry, with fear. Their eyes were flat and hard, without warmth, snakelike and glittering with a kind of latent cruelty, as if they might enjoy making someone suffer were it not such hard work. As Shah passed they leaned against the walls and made lazy malicious remarks and laughed. They were all men, all older than Michal, all swathed in rainbows. Their claws were long and shapely, and in some cases they were painted. They all looked as if they had not done a day's work in their lives.

Finally she lost patience with them, viciously sniggering and getting in her way, and rounded on a harlequin clutter of them nudging and giggling into extravagant sleeves like schoolgirls. She stopped and turned, and fixed the biggest and loudest of them with a stern eye and said, "Can you make that noise with your mouth as well?"

Michal stared at her in plain horror. The tall man leered. Like his nails, his face was painted. Gradually, as understanding dawned, the leer evolved perceptibly into a snarl and he swung his right arm, open-handed.

Shah slid into his mind and stopped him in mid-swing. With his attention focused on her and anger laying open his defences the penetration was easy. For long moments the big stretched-out form seemed to fill the corridor; then, slow as sunset, he collapsed, his arms and legs and head and chest folding and caving in under the incredulous gaze of his companions until he huddled on his knees on the floor, abject and shrunken like a gaudy discarded doll. The sniggering had ceased. Great tears rolled ponderously down the man's painted cheeks.

Shah slipped effortlessly back into her own brain and smiled condescendingly at the humiliated heap on the floor. "Don't cry, I forgive you," she said kindly, and turning her back on the silent gaping circle went her way with Michal bobbing in her wake like a rubber dinghy behind a schooner.

When they were out of sight the steward ventured unhappily, "Whatever you did there, you had better be good at it. You may have to do it again."

Shah shook her hair impatiently. She was annoyed: with the men, with Michal for not supporting her, mostly with herself for showing her hand. Her special perception would be the best weapon they had if she and Paul found themselves in conflict with the Mithraians: she cringed mentally in anticipation of Paul's scorn when he learned she had risked revealing herself to avoid a slap in the face. She told herself that the men were not clever enough to draw the right inferences from the encounter, that it was not important enough to lead to trouble, but still it rankled that she should make such a blunder on her first morning in the Hive. Her list of enemies was growing at an alarming rate.

"Anyway," she said to Michal, "who were those idiots?"

"The Hive's fighting men," replied the steward, watching her askance. "The one you – the one who – the one on the floor was Balrig, captain of Hornet Patrol."

"Fighting men?" exclaimed Shah, startled from self-reproach. "Michal, you have to be joking. Fighting men? – with paint on their faces and jewels in their ears, in frills and flounces most whores would consider vulgar? That lot couldn't fight their way out of a paper-bag!"

"No, well," Michal said defensively, "they have not had much practice lately."

"Then it's time they got some practice, because I have it on good authority there's a war coming."

Paul was hardly into his shirt when the hall door opened and closed again. He supposed Shah had come back for something, but in the living-room he found Amalthea, alone, turning slowly on her heel and viewing the apartment with a sardonic eye.

"In my part of the universe," Paul said levelly, "we knock. That way we don't get our heads blown off."

"In my city," said Amalthea with brittle humour, "I go where I please, and heads fall as and how I require. Are you comfortable here?" Like Michal, the lady had quickly taken in the fact that both bedrooms were in use.

"My wants are very simple. A jug of wine, a loaf of bread and four batteries of laser cannon homed in on anyone I have doubts about, and I can be comfortable most places."

Amalthea's blood-dark lips broadened in a crescent smile. "By heaven, I could have used you fifteen years ago."

"Is that how long you've been here?"

The lady's smile froze. "Who have you been talking to?"

Paul indulged in a little smile of his own. "You mean you don't know? I thought you were monitoring my every breath. In point of fact, no-one. But surely it isn't a secret, Amalthea – not from me?"

"You should address me –" she began icily, and then paused. "No, perhaps not. You may be the closest thing to an equal that I have. Use my name, before I forget it."

"And you must call me Paul," he said magnanimously.

Amalthea was strung between laughter and affront. "What do others call you?"

"Paul. Would I be right in supposing you are here to call me to a council of war, and the absence of my companion on walkabout is purely coincidental?"

The bloody crescent spread again. "Purely." She said the word with relish and made it sound like an obscenity.

Paul grinned. He indicated the door and followed her through it. He entertained a more than sneaking regard for terrible people: the ruthless, the strong, the wielders of power, the dictators of fates, the dark and the fierce and the free. It was more than half vanity. They reminded him of himself.

Round the perspex table in the dark chamber were arranged the Councillors of Mithras. Amalthea took a seat among them and waved Paul to another; her high place was vacant, her revolving chair discreetly removed. For the present she was happy to foster an illusion of equality.

Paul scanned the circle of faces impassively. They told him nothing. He needed Shah with her mind that saw through other minds to the roots of men's souls. He was a professional, skilled not only in the business of weaponry and tactics but also in the assessment of situations and of men. He knew his strengths and his limitations, and when to walk away, and how to do it without exposing his back. He was better equipped for negotiations such as these than almost anyone he had ever known. But since some very clever, frightened men had burned out of his brain the awesome power they had bred him for he had not had telepathy in his arsenal, and without it he felt blind. Having Shah beside him gave him an eye. Still, safety – his but more especially Shah's – depended on keeping private the nature of their relationship: he was resigned to managing without her, trusting in his ability to create an impression of confidence.

After Amalthea the senior Mithraian present was the lord Chaucer, Chancellor and Leader of the Council of Mithras, a tall broad powerful man in the full vigour of his age. He had full rosy cheeks and a glossy beard and dark, sumptuous clothes, and none of them said anything about him beside the steel-grey gimlet eyes sparkling, diamond bright and diamond hard, in the baby-pink creases of his face. The eyes were ageless, timeless, penetrating and perceptive as X-rays, knowing as a psychic's. When Paul met his gaze a kind of concussion seemed to echo through the silent room, as of an iron ram battering against an iron gate. For a long, suspenseful moment the tension reverberated between them, the lord's piercing scrutiny exactly matched by the mercenary's determined imperviousness, while the Councillors looked covertly and Amalthea candidly from one to the other, wondering which would crack first.

They were not to learn. This early confrontation was no more than a touching of feelers: the time was not yet ripe for a trial of strengths. Satisfied with the results of his first exploration, Chaucer veiled the probing challenge of his eyes with a smile. Paul's narrow face remained enigmatic; his expression, such as it was, did not flicker. But he felt like a man who has survived a conflict rather than won one.

Amalthea, with the air of a fox supervising a cockfight, her purple eyes heavy and ambivalent as wine, leaned forward slightly and tapped the table-top and called the meeting to order.

Shah was still looking for real people. Despairing of finding any among the pleasure arcades or the opulent public salons where the languid gaudy men gathered to drink heady liqueurs that made them more raucous, more ill-natured and less like the warrior élite of a vital culture than ever, she had insisted on Michal extending his itinerary to take in the manufacturing and service plants in the remote basements of the Hive. There she found Drones. They were no more real to her than the fighting men and, in their dismal apathy and bovine acceptance of their drudgery, hardly less irritating.

Michal tried to explain the Drones. "They are of a different people. They are very stupid. If we did not feed them they would sit under the trees and starve to death. If we give them work, and oversee them, they can carry out simple tasks and then we feed them and their families. They look miserable and half-dead working in our factories and maintenance areas. But they also look miserable and half-dead sitting under the trees, and then they are hungry too."

"Were the Drones here when the Hive people came?" asked Shah. Michal shot her a sharp, hunted look and said nothing. "When was that?" she persisted.

The steward was patently uncomfortable. Had there been more than just the two of them leaning on their elbows on the rail of the walkway overlooking the factory floor, where the Drones with their wood-brown faces dragged themselves round with a lack of industry or any enthusiasm, even for revolt, that made Shah want to kick some life into them, she would have thought he feared spies. He shrugged and fidgeted and finally said, "I do not know."

Shah smiled at him, which made him more uncomfortable still. "Don't be silly, Michal, of course you know. Were you born here, or were you on the ship that brought your people?"

He stared. "How could I have been born here? I was a page in the lady's household and she brought me on her vessel. It was perhaps fifteen years ago. Please do not tell anyone I spoke of it. Please can we speak of something else?"

At which unsatisfactory juncture Shah had to let the matter rest, or risk alienating her only Mithraian friend. Turning away she gave his arm a comradely pat, and felt the small muscles jump beneath his smooth skin; and then something she had not expected touched her brain and she received a sudden overwhelming impression of greenery and growth, crowding, not threatening but somehow affectionate, fraternal. For a split second she was as a forest tree. Then the vision was gone, leaving her gasping. She had no idea where the image had come from. Her mind reeling, she staggered back against the rail and stared out over the slowly labouring half-wits. It seemed inconceivable that one of those grey-garbed somnambulists was host to a telepath's brain. Yet she knew Michal was not, a quick scan confirmed that none of the overseers was, and there was no-one else. Marginally conscious that Michal was regarding her with concern growing to alarm, too occupied for the moment to try to reassure him, she spread wide the portals of her remarkable mind in an effort to pick up on the communication again.

But though the background hum of thoughts that was her perennial companion was amplified and fractured into its individual patterns – whirling, confused agitation from the man beside her, bad-tempered boredom from the overseers, and from the Drones a monotone level of thought just one step up from utter vacancy, like blue-green cyanophytes wondering whether to invent sex and, if so, what it might be good for – the green thought was gone beyond her powers to follow. For a moment she felt, as well as startled past measure, bereft. It was as if someone had of a sudden malice hacked down all that green and loving forest and left her parching alone.

Awareness that Michal was clucking and fluttering and in imminent danger of laying an egg on the walkway brought her back to herself. She leaned against him, getting her breath back, letting the physical contact steady them both.

Michal's virgin heart hammered its way gradually back towards its normal rhythm; not quite reaching it, however, for the soft pressure of her body against him resulted in an aberration of pulse and a congestion about his breast-bone that had nothing to do with fright. "Lady, what happened?"

Shah raised her head weakly and grinned. "Nothing. Really," she lied. "Just one of those little wobbly turns women are prone to. You know."

"No," said Michal, interestedly.

Chapter Three

Paul dreamed. He did not often dream, but when the phantasms came they made up in spectacle what they lacked in frequency. All his dreams were nightmares.

Great amorphous shapes he could not identify were feeding on him. They stabbed him with knives and lapped his blood. He could not move. They were accusing him of something. He did not understand. They stabbed him anyway, and all the time his life was slowly ebbing from the wounds he was trying to understand why but they would not explain. They did not care whether he understood or not, as long as he died.

He woke sweating, fighting off the clammy sheet, wide-eyed and looking for blood. He found Shah's long arms around his sweat-slick body, holding him while the terror-spasms subsided to let him drag clean air into his cringing lungs. His face was grey, and under the fringe of his sodden hair his eyes were vastly dilated, the gold-flecked irises compacted to narrow brilliant coronas.

Shah said gently, "Better now?"

Still in the compass of her arms he nodded fitfully. "Hell roast, though," he whispered, "that was a classic."

"Tell me." He told her, too weak not to. "You're right," she said, finally releasing him. "That was a classic."

"Did I wake you?"

"No, I sit up every night on the off-chance of you being attacked by large shapeless things with knives." Paul chuckled shakily. Shah disappeared into the kitchen and returned with hot drinks. "It's nearly day. You don't want to go back to sleep, do you?"

"Not enormously."

"Because brother, do I have some news for you."

"I too have tidings," offered Paul. "You were asleep when I got back and I didn't want to get you up."

"What made you change your mind?"

He grinned tiredly. "A man isn't responsible for his dreams. I just happen to have a vivid imagination."

"You have a violent soul," said Shah disapprovingly. "I suppose your news is that you've reached agreement with Amalthea over the financial arrangements for blasting some poor unsuspecting sod out of the sky."

"Well," Paul observed thoughtfully into his mug, "sods they may be, and unsuspecting they maybe and hopefully remain, but that note of sympathy is conspicuously absent from most people's voices when they talk about pirates. It is specifically and totally absent from the voices of pirates' victims."

"These people? Maybe they're victims. Maybe they're pretty like pirates themselves. This planet was occupied when they came here. Maybe the Drones aren't anybody's idea of an evolutionary zenith, but they are human and they've been forced into the rôle of slave-labourers." She told him about the basement regions far beneath them supplying the Hive with all its corporate needs. "Which brings me to my news. Paul, somewhere here there's a telepath." She explained.

The revelation rocked Paul almost as hard as it had hit Shah. Each was the other's only experience ever of another mind-delver, and Paul's faculties had been destroyed. The discovery of one on Mithras was thrilling and alarming to approximately equal degrees: exciting, especially for Shah, because of the prospect of a unique communion; dangerous if their only real advantage and therefore their safety margin were to be eroded by an equivalent facility operating on behalf of the Hive.

Paul's first thoughts shot to the lord Chaucer with his knowing diamond eyes, because telepathy reinforcing that psyche was what he feared most – even more than cruel, arrogant but divinable Amalthea. But he was sure it was neither of them. Shah had met Amalthea, and Paul did not believe that Chaucer could have turned mind-rays on him without his knowledge. He had recognised Shah's ability the moment he saw her, and her first venture into his brain had been as painful as an excavation. Though he retained no perception of his own, his brain-cells were preternaturally sensitive: before him no-one had ever felt or sensed or suspected Shah's exploration of their minds.

Yet if the telepath was one of the Hive people, he should by every rule of caution and common sense have been at that Council meeting. Paul could hardly remember some of the faces, but there was no doubt in his mind that any of them masked a perception. The telepath was either unknown to the Hive or outside it. That was intriguing, possibly disturbing, but not a cause for concern. Paul's response was less enthusiastic than Shah's because he had less to gain and more to lose from contact with even a benign telepath. He could not share in any communion and he was afraid of losing Shah to an unflawed perceptive.

"What are you thinking of doing about it?"

Shah frowned, not understanding his coolness. "Look for him, of course. If I can pick up his mind again I may I get a fix on him. Otherwise I'm going to look outside. I There was a strong feeling of outside in the image I got."

"We don't even know what is outside – not beyond the clearing. I don't think the Hive people go into the forest."

"Then perhaps it's time somebody did," Shah retorted tartly. "I'll see what Michal will tell me. You can ask 'Gyr' for a scan. If that's not too much trouble."

Paul stiffened. "No trouble. But I shan't have time to come exploring with you. You'll have to be careful."

"Don't worry, I'll be well looked after. I have one devoted slave already and I expect to collect more. That's my other bit of news. Apart from the sorry specimens in the Drone community, it appears that Amalthea and I are the only women on this planet. The Hive people were the crew of a fleet vessel carrying the Empress to an outpost of her system. There was a malfunction and they drifted for four years before arriving here. They expected to effect repairs and leave, but we were right about the atmosphere – it ate their ship or something. The point is, there is no generation here. Everyone you see was on that ship when it embarked 19 years ago, and they're all men. Michal was Amalthea's page: he's the youngest person in the Hive.

"And that," she said, rising and walking away with a backward glance that was half provocative, half earnest, "makes me something special round here." She closed the door smartly behind her.

Paul rested his arms across his raised knees and his chin on his arms and watched the closed door for a long time. His flecked obsidian eyes smouldered like embers. "You think I don't know?"

They walked out to the shuttle. Shah invited Michal along. He went, because he would go with her into any Hades of his heart's imagining, and gladly, because Paul walked with a traveller's stride that carried him ahead and left the young man and the girl to follow at their own pace; but outside the Hive was a place of fear to him, and all the way from the tall fluted gates to the bare swathe where the shuttle shone in its constantly retouched coat of oil he was glancing anxiously around him, measuring the distance from the Hive and the distance remaining to the small haven of the waiting craft. In total the trip was a scant mile, but to Michal who had spent most of his life within close confines it felt an epic journey. Beyond the naked earth the forest began.

When Shah and the steward reached the shuttle Paul was already on board, seated at the console and keying instructions to "Gyr's" main computer, a hundred miles up and half a planet away. While they waited for a reply he ran a damage check which showed the oil to be serving its function well.

The men painting the shuttle were Drones under the guidance of a single Hive overseer. Michal wondered how he could bear to work this close to the trees. The Drones, of course, were happier out here than anywhere else, though their enthusiasm was ever a low-key affair. They just slouched a little more jauntily. Painting an inert lump of metal with oil, and starting again at the nose whenever they reached the tail, was the exact task for which they were fitted by Providence. The high spot of their day came when the oil-can ran dry, and one of their number was despatched up to the Hive to replenish it. More often than not some distraction would waylay him and a second Drone would be sent to bring him back. Sometimes a third Drone would be needed to find the second Drone.

Despite Shah's misgivings, the Hive people did not abuse the Drones. This was less due to their kind and generous natures than to the total pointlessness of trying to beat sense into the apathetic things. A belaboured Drone would sit down beneath the lash and die without a sound or any sign of displeasure, nor would his relatives learn anything at all useful from his demise. It had occasionally happened that overseers, their patience strained beyond human tolerances, had cracked under the strain and pounded disinterested Drones to a bloody pulp, but experience showed that the only way for a supervisor to retain his sanity in the face of such provocation was for him to treat his charges as oxen: strong and biddable but quite mindless and basically ineducable. He would feed and water them, and harness and direct their strength, and he might grow a little fond of them particularly if his team seemed less slow, stupid or trying than another man's, but he would never ever think of them as people. There was no way of knowing how they thought of him.

When the console began chattering back "Gyr's" response, to his amazement and acute embarrassment tears sprang to Michal's eyes. Concerned as he had been for her, Shah took his hand.

"Whatever's the matter?"

"I – I do not know," he stumbled, rubbing his sleeve furiously across his eyes. "Forgive me! I – that sound – the last time I heard it –"

Shah understood. "Was fifteen years ago, on your own ship, before you were marooned."

"I suppose – It is silly – I am sorry. Oh God," he moaned, squirming in an agony of self-consciousness.

Shah laughed and hugged him. "Don't take on so. Everybody gets nostalgic sometimes – even him." She nodded at Paul. "If you want to see tears in his eyes, ask him about camels."

"Camels?"

"He used to breed them. He had this big bull, and a cow he used to talk to as if it was his mother."

"Camels?"

"You know: big sandy-coloured things with humps."

"Humps?"

The communication chattered to an end. Paul folded a slip of paper into his pocket. "Well, that's 'Gyr's' assessment of the situation, but I don't know if you're going to like it."

"Well? Tell us the worst."

"Now?" Paul raised a not very tactful eyebrow in Michal's direction.

Michal, already distressed, reddened and drew himself up stiffly. "You have matters to discuss. I will wait outside." He rushed to the airlock, and it closed on him with a crisp, quiet click that seemed to reverberate longer than a slam.

"That was a bit unnecessary," said Shah, smarting on his behalf.

Paul glowered at her from under low brows. "That isn't a lap-dog you've picked up. He's Amalthea's servant, and however enamoured he may be of you he's going to jump to her bidding because she's spent twenty years training him that way. Every word he hears will find its way back to her, and I'm not so fond of the woman or so impressed by her honesty that I care to share my secrets with her."

"I don't believe Michal spies on us," Shah retorted hotly. "And I see no danger in sharing with him the results of a geographical survey of a world he's lived on for fifteen years."

"I'll make a deal with you," said Paul snidely. "I won't guess what people are thinking if you won't guess what's likely to prove dangerous."

"Don't offer me your deals, Paul, I know what they're worth. You tell me you've made one with Amalthea, but you act as if she's the devil's mother. If she isn't, that makes you a pretty nasty bastard; and if she is, I'd rather not think what that makes you."

"I'll tell you what I'm not. I'm not naïve enough to suppose that because somebody I don't know from Adam wants to hire me they necessarily want to pay me as well. I think I've built enough safeguards into this deal you so despise that when I'm finished here we'll get away with both our money and our lives. But if you are stupid enough to place your trust in Amalthea or Michal or anyone else on this planet, there'll be a series of unfortunate accidents involving falling masonry or unmarked quicksands or guns that go off as we're cleaning them, and Mithras will have a nice new battleship for the price of an exploding medal and three inches of fuse."

"Don't worry," snapped Shah, "you've done a good job on me. I trust no-one, on this planet or any other. I don't even trust you."

It was not true, but Paul thought it was. He stared at her, angry and hurt; then he threw the slip of paper, tight crumpled from his fist, on the deck at her feet. He locked quickly through the hatches and went stalking back towards the Hive.

Michal waited a cautious minute, looking this way and that, before returning on board. He found Shah on her knees on the deck, carefully smoothing out the screw of paper with its innocuous information that had laid all she cared about in ruins, while large slow tears slid down her cheeks.

At his footfall she lifted her face and smiled at him, tragedy bright in her eyes. "You see? Nostalgia can make fools of us all."

Michal's experience of women may have been limited, but his instincts were good. He said, "I slipped in the oil and hurt my ankle. You would not have a bandage?"

She found one in a plastic box with a red cross on it. By the time she had applied it to her complete satisfaction she had regained mastery of herself. She patted his strapped ankle as she might have patted a dog and rolled his trouser-leg down over it; and Michal, leaning forward with sudden, impetuous urgency, caught her wrists in his hands and her eyes in his solemn, intense gaze. "Lady –"

"Shah," she said, not for the first time.

"Shah. Please, do not let us come between you."

She shook her head very slightly. "I don't understand."

"I am not a spy," hissed Michal, gripping her still. "I do not know what is between you and Paul. But I do know my world and my people, and all of Mithras would not weigh as a falling leaf beside the things you share. There is nothing and no-one here worth risking your happiness for."

He finally released her hands, but neither of them moved. Touched, Shah murmured, "Michal, what can you possibly know of my happiness?"

He almost laughed. "Sweet heaven, lady, I have read less in long books than in your face when Paul is near you. When he enters a room you glow sun-bright, and when he leaves that glow fades. I believe this is – love?"

It was a moment before Shah answered, and then her voice was low. "It is. But still it has little to do with happiness."

"I would not know. Here there is neither. Shah, do not stay. Make him take you away, before –" He stopped abruptly.

"Before?"

Michal's face wrung. "My life, if a word of this should reach the lady Amalthea –"

"It won't. Michal, are we in danger here?"

He shook his head. His eyes were fraught. "I do not know. Truly, Shah, I would tell you if I did. I know of no plot against you – but –"

Shah tried his mind and found it ingenuous. He had a child's conscience. There was no deceit in him. She liked him. Whatever Paul said, she trusted him. "But?"

"Try to understand. The Hive is not a real community, growing and developing as real communities do through the making of families and the rearing of children. In its present form our culture has no future. We have wealth and comfort and art, and the leisure to enjoy these things, but if we stay on Mithras the people of the Hive will be extinct in fifty years, leaving the place to the Drones who were here before we came. That is a bitter truth to contemplate, and it makes my people bitter too: angry and bitter and uncaring. We behave as people with a future do not. I do not know what will become of us, but I fear that if you stay you will become cruel and uncaring too. I do not know if my people would hurt you. I believe Amalthea will use you, if she can. But more than that, I fear that Mithras will make you as it made us. Here even hard metal is corrupted."

"It has to be admitted," Amalthea told Paul, her tone humorous, her eyes calculating, "that greed was the main reason for our predicament. We came to Mithras because there were materials we needed to repair our star-drive system. When we found there were other materials that we wanted –" she flashed her jewelled fingers under his nose – "avarice persuaded us to stay and garner them, and by the time we were satisfied with our crop it was no longer possible for us to leave."

The first explosive malfunction aboard the frigate "Galactic Dragon" had plunged her into uncharted regions far beyond Amalthea's archipelago empire. Like a wandering asteroid she drifted down the dark tunnel of superspace until, velocity slowly leeching away to entropy, she was finally spewed out into a new galaxy with alien suns and, at length, a small green planet whose spectograph promised rare minerals to heal the damaged systems.

"Galactic Dragon" took up a parking orbit around the world they called Mithras while surface parties went down in landers. They found wonderful things. Their reports brought the Empress herself and almost everyone else down to Mithras in every serviceable tender.

They found gems as big as eggs nestling in the roots of trees or peeping strabismically out of the rocks. They found nuggets of gold and nodules of silver strewn casually along the banks and beds of streams. They found diamond-pipes prolific as conveyor-belts, spilling out rivers of blue clay and white fire. They found they had only to take an afternoon's stroll with a few hand-tools in a sack to return rich beyond the wildest of their very wild dreams.

They found that by the time they thought of going back to "Galactic Dragon" with the minerals needed to repair her, the small craft which were their only link with her had incubated a strange leprosy in the damp sweet air. Their outer skins had rotted into holes, and in their delicate inner workings cogs tooled to within a thousandth of an inch were dissolving into a thick metallic soup.

Amalthea remembered, still vivid after fifteen years, standing with her chief engineer in the bowels of her personal barge and listening to the slow drip of corruption all around her. None of the many craft that had put down on Mithras ever left it.

For some years, as trapped in their orbiting prison as were the landing parties below, the skeleton crew left aboard "Galactic Dragon" circled aimlessly in their crippled ark. Then the pull of a stray comet so elongated the ellipse of her track that she broke away from Mithras and went once more wandering in the void and was not seen again.

For most of the Mithraians the loss of the "Dragon" signalled the end of their hope. While their mother-ship had held station with the planet, capable of sending radio messages to any other nomads who might chance along, they enshrined the expectation of ultimate rescue. They yoked the Drones and built the Hive, and went on collecting jewels and precious metals until the treasure occupied all available space, in the firm belief that this year or next, or the one after that, they would be discovered and conveyed back to some civilisation which would put a proper value on the fruits of their labours.

The loss of their radio beacon destroyed that hope. Just as surely as they had once believed rescue inevitable, now they believed it impossible. In deepest despair, they would have lain down and died, or killed one another for the distraction, had not the Empress Amalthea taken the situation in hand. It was her iron will that kept them building and working long after a Hive capable of meeting their requirements was complete, and it was her intuition that drove the engineers and science officers from the "Galactic Dragon" in pursuit of a radio system employing hard gems and soft metals.

Their success after more than a decade of endeavour enabled Amalthea to send the message that would end the isolation of the Hive people. But almost none of them understood why she had summoned not a passenger ship but a battle-cruiser.

"Pirates," said Amalthea. "It was entirely in keeping with our luck so far that the first distress signal broadcast by our new transmitter should be intercepted by someone whose preferred solution to our problem was to put us out of our misery. They first came a year ago. We beat them off. Four months later they were back; more of them. This time we bought them off – the alternative was having the Hive destroyed about our ears. I paid them tribute: I, an empress.

"They said they would return for the next instalment when we had had time to collect it. I knew they would return; but I will not be humbled before them a second time. I kept signalling. Finally my message reached you. I will gladly pay what they would take, because when you blast their ship all over this spiral arm the shock-waves will keep anyone else from ever trying the same thing. I want an explosion that will be heard clear across the galaxy, Paul. Then we will think of leaving here, with our belongings, in our own good time."

"You want me to blow them out of the sky? I can do it, but that way you won't get your tribute back."

Amalthea eyed him sharply. "What are you saying – that you can capture their ship?"

"Unless they prefer to die."

The Empress bristled. "They will die anyway."

"So long as you don't tell them that while they still have the choice."

Her pale brow, smooth and soft as vellum, wrinkled quizzically. "Does it not bother you that I am proposing to massacre men from whom you have wrung a submission?"

"Not enormously. I don't care that much what happens to people who prey on defenceless settlers." He grinned suddenly. "To be entirely frank, I don't care all that much more what happens to the defenceless settlers."

Amalthea laughed richly. "As long as it does not happen while they owe you money. I admire ruthlessness, Paul. I just hope you fight as hard as you talk."

Paul shrugged. "If I don't win, you don't have to pay me."

"If you do not win, I expect there to be nothing left to pay."

Shah and Michal were still in the shuttle. Neither was anxious to return to the Hive, of for different reasons. Shah was turning the communication from "Gyr" in her hands. To say it had caused such trouble, it was a non-committal sort of thing.

Michal nodded at it. "Can you tell me what it says?"

Shah looked up, a little vaguely. "Mm? Oh – yes, of course, there's nothing in the least bit sensitive about it. It says there is no evidence of settlements anywhere on the planet except here, but that small groups – Drone families? – are scattered fairly evenly across the surface with a slight increase in density in the neighbourhood of the Hive. It found no indications of building except here and no sign of technology except here. In short, it agrees with Amalthea: the only Mithraians worth talking about are the Hive people."

"I could have told you that," said Michal.

"Yes, but you could have been mistaken."

"Is it important?"

For a moment she considered telling him about herself and the image she had received; but Paul's wishes weighed more heavily with her than a mere whim or inclination of her own. She was also conscious that what Michal did not know he could not be pressed for: she was less afraid of his betraying her to Amalthea than that he might suffer at the Empress's hands rather than do so.

"Not important. But I'm curious. We aren't all space travellers from earliest childhood. My experience of worlds is very limited – I want to see something of this one. The Hive's impressive, but it's not all Mithras. I want to know what else there is here. I want to see how the Drones live, and what kind of trees they sit under. I want to see what colour the sunsets are, and whether there is a Milky Way when the moons go down. I want to see if maybe your rainbows are straight. Come on." She jumped up, grabbing his hand. "Let's go for a walk."

Michal stared at her, appalled. "A walk? Out there? By the trees?"

"Into the trees," Shah said firmly. "But only if you want to."

He exhaled, relieved. "Good. I do not."

"Then I'll see you back at the Hive, later."

"No!" Michal shouldered his trepidation like a physical burden. "No. I will come."

Chapter Four

Michal did not know why he was so afraid. He was too young to remember with any clarity the settlers' early ventures into the forest, and tales of them were not spoken. All he knew was that once the great clearing had been made and the Hive begun no-one from the "Galactic Dragon" essayed the woods again. The trees were not forbidden them: there was no need, people were only too happy to stay within the fastness of their own compound. Everything they needed was there: mines and brickfields and hydroponic farms that grew all their food. The clearing was all their world. If a particularly shiftless Drone decided he had had enough of servitude and slunk back into the trees, no-one followed: there was no shortage of Drones ready to trade labour of a kind for easy meals. In the forest they lived as gatherers, working harder for less food than they did as serfs of the Hive. There were no Hive children to stray into the crowding thicket. Amalthea's empire now was a cleared circle that a man could cross in an hour and walk round in half a day, with the high broad dome of the Hive looming, vastly out of proportion to its surroundings, at the centre.

Fields and tanks fringed the great structure, where worked most of those Mithraians whose duties took them outside, supervising small armies of toiling field-Drones. The fields extended almost to the naked no-man's-land where Paul had landed the shuttle. Also clustered towards the perimeter were the mine-workings – after fifteen years the Mithraians had been reduced to digging for their treasures – a number of small oil-wells, brick kilns and hamlets of long low shelters where the Drones lived. None of these structures encroached upon the earth break: the Hive people did not expect invasion from the forest but nor did they propose to provide cover for anything coming that way. The break was continually scoured of all vegetation, and supervising the work was the most unpopular task in the Hive, for it took the overseers into closer proximity with the forest than any of their colleagues. There was no perimeter fence as such, but the sunlight reaching under the edgemost trees grew a dense thicket of mixed greenery like an unbroken circular hedge.

Pushing through that hedge in the wake of an alien girl whose curiosity amounted in the circumstances almost to insanity, who had neither a notion what they might encounter beyond it nor any obvious means of dealing with danger, was the bravest thing Michal had ever done. But his whirling emotions would have been in yet greater turmoil if he had known how Shah's nerves were leaping beneath her guise of self-confidence. Paul would have seen the too-bright eyes, the too-quick smile, the excessive resolution in the set of her wide shoulders, the subtle over-animation of her long body, and would have known; but Paul was not there.

Shah knew the fringing thicket was not an impenetrable barrier because she knew from Michal that the Drones passed through it between their long houses in the compound and their spiritual home among the trees. But she could find no actual opening, and when she pitted herself against it bodily the dense weave of its twigs and tendrils held her like a net. She fought its resistance with bare hands and a kind of loathing, already regretting deeply the impulse that had brought her here. She did not fear the forest as Michal did, but her thoughts dwelt on Paul, angry and upset back at the Hive, and her scratched hands and torn clothes and the whip-weals across her cheeks seemed a high price to pay for indulging her spite against him. She wished she had not lost her temper. She wished she could abandon her exploration, at least for the moment, and go and straighten things out between them.

Had she been alone she would undoubtedly have done so. Having Michal in tow made it harder. If she turned back now he would never believe that the evil ambience of the forest had not finally got to her too, and rather than ridding him of his dread she would confirm it eternally. She would never get him this far again if they turned back now. She had promised him a walk in the woods, and whatever his inclinations and her own she felt obliged to deliver. Paul's hurts and hers would have to wait. They both had enough old scars to know how to bear new ones. She plugged on.

All at once, with the sound in her ears of Michal struggling through the tangle behind her like something ferocious on her trail, Shah was conscious of the thicket yielding to her, surrendering its tenacious grasp on her and letting her pass. She staggered through its last defences almost without hindrance and emerged, sweaty and scraped and breathless with effort, into a wider place. She bent hands on knees over her heaving chest to give her labouring lungs a chance to recover.

Not until a minute later did she realise that Michal, who had been panting on her heels like a spent hound all through the clawing hedge, had not emerged from it in her wake. She straightened up and looked round for him. She called his name. There was no reply. She sent her perception in search of him.

She found his faithful, uncomplicated mind in a state of numb terror and thought for a moment he had succumbed to claustrophobia amid the crowding scrub. She called, "Come on – the last bit's the easiest." Then as his mind started to slip out of focus she understood what was happening to him. She plunged back into the tangle and found him halfway to his knees, his eyes closing, hands pawing slackly at the green noose choking him.

Strong with desperation, Shah's hands fought the clinging tendrils away from Michal's throat, and as, released, he dropped she grabbed his wrist and dragged him clear of the thicket and out onto the forest floor.

Feeling the mumbling of his brain as he lay grey-faced at her feet, Shah was not afraid that she had been too late, but she was aware that she could have been. She knelt down and rolled him over on his side, and listened to his starved lungs whoop in the damp air, and watched him claw half-sensibly at his raw bruised throat, and wondered what had actually happened.

The hedgerow was high and thick and densely tangled with

groping, trailing branches and tendrils, and it was possible that in trying to force a way through it Michal had managed to enmesh himself and, panicking, had succeeded in drawing the living ropes tighter as he strove to get free. Given his acute nervousness about the whole green world beyond the scorched earth perimeter, it was perfectly possible. But she did not believe it. It had happened too quickly, for one thing, and for another it was a little too convenient that just as her problems had ended Michal's had taken so dramatic a turn for the worse. Yet if ill chance were not responsible, she could not imagine what was.

"That thing attacked me," Michal whispered hoarsely. He was shaking visibly as he knelt facing her, propped up on his fists. His eyes were shocked and accusing, bright coals in black pits in the ashy frame of his face.

Shah shook her head. "It couldn't have. It was only a bush."

"It attacked me," insisted the frightened man.

Shah shook her head again, smiling, but a tiny perplexed frown between her eyebrows reflected an unease she could not shake off and the absurd inclination to take his panicky imaginings at face value. At last, still wondering, she looked around.

It was a very strange forest, although Shah – who was raised in a desert land and had less experience of trees than Michal – did not appreciate its curiosity. It seemed unable to make up its mind what kind of forest it was. Tall slender trees like firs rubbed shoulders with broad gnarled trees like olives. Roots like the groins of cathedrals raised trees like great mangroves proud of the forest floor, which was littered with giant cones and deep in leaf-mould. The grey boles of the trees were strides apart and they carried a high canopy of light-splintering foliage which blotted out the sky.

There was no more agreement on the season than on the nature of the forest. Some of the trees were in blossom, sprawling powder-puffs of white or blue foam clouding the high tops and lying misty on the ground below. Some were turning to gold, or shedding hosts of bronze leaves which swam in deep drifts down the woodland avenues. The air was sweetly cloying, and had the greenhouse taste of having been breathed too much. So far below the canopy there was no breeze to stir and freshen it. Its damp pungency was redolent of slow decay. There was no birdsong in the branches, no furry scuttering among the roots. Not even the whirr of insects disturbed the soft, waiting silence of the eerie uncanny wood.

Shah had an extraordinary, compelling sensation of the wood waiting for her response to what had happened in the thicket.

Conscious that she could be making a fool of herself, aware too that the only one who could see her was Michal and he was in no mood for laughing, she asked for his knife. Wide-eyed, expectant as the trees, he produced a broad leaf-shaped blade from a tooled sheath at his belt. He could never remember using it except to peel fruit for Amalthea: the fighting men, who scrapped among themselves viciously at times, left the Empress's steward strictly alone.

Shah took it, steeling herself to its weight and feel, and selecting a sappy young tree like a rubber plant stabbed it deliberately in the bole. As she wrenched the knife from the bleeding wound she directed stern thoughts of reproof and the intention to stand no nonsense from a stack of kindling on a broad front into the grey forest twilight.

Immediately, before she was ready, flashed back the rich green emission she had first experienced in the bowels of the Hive. Then it had nearly knocked her over: now, coming as it seemed to from all around her, it both blasted and supported her and she felt she could hardly have fallen had she tried.

Her first instinct was to cringe away from it, to shut fast the portals of her mind against the monstrous, insufferable invasion. But she fought the impulse, and with an almost physical effort opened wide, petal-like, the psychic flanges that guarded her mentality. The green thought flooded in like a tide, and in her head took shape and reason and spoke to her with tongues she could fathom though they made neither words nor sounds. As she listened she began to understand; and what she was beginning to understand was staggering.

Michal broke into her import-laden reverie. At his voice the vision and all the other sensory communications which were accumulating to turn her picture of Mithras on its head vanished, and the sudden loss of them made her wheel angrily on him. He was still kneeling on the ground in the sun-dappled half-light and he was pointing. "Look," he said again.

A Drone had walked through the thicket hedge as if it were his garden gate. For a long minute he stood regarding them even as they watched him, all unspeaking. Then he calmly turned and went on his way. Amid the tall trees and the broad trees and the soft grey light, his slow and measured stride – which seemed in the open fields a stupid, indolent shamble – took on a dignity and an aptness to his environment. He looked as if he could keep up his careful, silent pace all the day that the forest world knew. His short lumpish body, brown of limb and grey of garb, blended with the sturdy grey-brown trunks and threw off the watcher's gaze long before he disappeared from their sight.

"Do you know him?" Shah found herself whispering.

Michal stared at her as he had stared at the Drone. "It was a Drone. Shah, there are thousands of the dreary things –"

"– And to you they all look alike," she finished irritably. "Michal, my son, do I have news for you." But she did not deliver it then. She caught his hand, which was still vaguely pointing into the trees, and pulled him to his feet. "Come on, we're going to follow him."

Michal was reluctant to follow the unknown Drone into the unknown wood, but he was even less inclined to stay or attempt to return through the thicket alone, so he did as he was bid. If it struck him as ironic that in a world virtually without women he still managed to be hen-pecked, he must have decided that now was not the moment to assert his masculinity.

Paul was working with star-charts and logarithms at the dining-room table when he heard the clatter of running feet in the corridor. For a split second his internal organs seemed to cling together in fear. Then he put down his pen and rose quietly and moved to the front door. He opened it to the first fall of the hammering fist.

It was not a murder squad but a messenger from the lord Chaucer. Paul snatched his charts and calculations from the table before following the man at a sprint.

He found the Chancellor poring over a chip of green light pulsing on a dark plastic screen in the radio-room. The display, like everything else in the small high room, hunched under the curving shoulder of the Hive and inferior only to Amalthea's cell and the golden hall, was not only home-made but home-conceived. Ingenuity amounting to genius had gone into the design of devices employing the higher physics but none of the harder metals. Nothing in the room seemed familiar to Paul, even with the vague once-removed familiarity of unknown scions of known families, but when he studied the jewelled dials and silver and plastic consoles he was able to identify their functions, and he was impressed more than he would have admitted at how few gaps remained in the array. The Mithraians had developed a whole unconventional technology to replace that standard one which the hungry atmosphere had eaten away.

He was not allowed long for contemplation. Chaucer, leaning his heavy body on his hands over the screen, looked up with that unholy luminescence men call battle-light in his diamond eyes. He tapped the emerald spot with an immaculately manicured claw. "That is them," he declared, smiling in his beard, a note of triumph in his deep equivocal voice.

"You're sure?" Paul could feel the nerves and muscles all through his body keying up in readiness for combat. He was not afraid. He had been bred for a soldier, raised to it, and though he no longer enjoyed the massive advantage that had been bred into him his practical and tactical skills continued to increase with every exercise of them. He was that ideal fighting machine, a robot with imagination. Still his chemistry was that of a man, and when action offered adrenalin flowed, reminding him that he was mortal.

Chaucer flayed him with an impatient glance. "Of course I am sure. Who else? This is hardly a spatial highway; if we got any passing traffic we would not have been here fifteen years. Besides, I know that signal. Look." He pulled a drawing across the screen. "That is their ship. It is a semi-armed merchantman they have picked up from somewhere, but there is nothing half-hearted about their armament now."

"Do you know their capabilities?"

"Roughly." He read out a string of numbers. Paul jotted them down beside his own calculations.

"What's the calibration on that screen?" He flicked through his log tables. "Then intercept is about here –" he pointed with his pen – "which is handy enough. It'll be dark by then, you'll be able to watch. I'll go up to 'Gyr' now, but I'm going to hug the planet as long as I can. I've a lot more power than them, I can afford to, and the less time they have to work out what to do about me the better."

"Very well." Chaucer looked at him sideways. "The lady told me you could capture their ship."

Paul chose to misunderstand. "When were you talking to Shah?"

The Chancellor smiled thinly. "My apologies. I have not yet adjusted to the change in circumstances. The lady Amalthea said you could take the ship undamaged."

"Hardly undamaged. Intact perhaps, if they prefer to take their chances with you than with me."

"It is not only that we wish to recover our treasure. A ship of our own, even one we had to repair, would make us immeasurably freer than we are now."

"I'll bear it in mind," grunted Paul. "Now, if you'll excuse me –"

"I am coming with you," said Chaucer.

Paul's narrow jaw dropped. "Like hell you are!"

The lord of Mithras caught his wrist in a grip Paul could not break. His diamond eyes were savage; Paul was startled at the strength of him, the power of that massive personality which bore down on him like a heavy weight. The beautiful voice was descended to the awesome hiss of a labouring machine that brooks no hindrance.

"It is not given to many to deny me, mercenary, and you are not one. My people have bought you with years of waiting and working, with fear and faith and a truly unreasonable belief in the future, and I will not leave their investment and perhaps their last hope in the hands of a paid assassin I do not know and have no cause to trust.

"Look at you. Do you know how we have kept the Hive together the last half-year, Amalthea and I? We have presented you to our people, gift-wrapped. We have made you out a Titan – an invincible. They trusted in us for nineteen years and finally we failed them. So we gave them you to trust instead, and it was trust only that kept them from falling into despair, schism, conflict and ultimate self-destruction. The promise of you was their salvation.

"And then you arrive: one man, with a ship they can't see, and a whore they can, who talks more about money than fighting. It is not what they were led to expect. You have to prove yourself to them if you are to justify my actions and those of the lady Amalthea. Our credibility is riding on you. So when the guns flare and your precious hull staggers under their pounding, you will not be tempted to turn tail and find elsewhere an easier way of making money because I shall be there to stop you. If we do not win this battle, Paul, I shall not want to survive it and you will not get the choice."

Paul's voice was low, flat. "Take your hand off me."

Chaucer could not remember ever in his life being threatened. Even Amalthea found other ways. But he had the distinct feeling he was being threatened now. "What?"

"Take your hand off me."

The Chancellor loomed over the smaller man, and his lip curled. The silence in the close dim room was avid. Chaucer tightened his grip until he felt the bones grate; then, with elaborate distaste, he threw Paul's arm back at him. The sneer and the derisive gesture were for the benefit of the people watching. Inwardly he felt neither anger nor contempt, only a passing respect for a solitary alien ready to oppose him in his own stronghold, surrounded by his own men, and some anxiety lest he should have underestimated the mercenary in his delicate and finely tooled calculations. He felt, like a twinge of indigestion, a regret that he had not had more time to consolidate his assessment of this fiercely unbending young man on whom all his clever, tortuous planning pivoted.

Unbending still, dark marks on his wrist but no pain in his face or voice, Paul was speaking through his teeth. "I told Amalthea, and now I'll tell you, and after that I don't expect to have to say it again. I do this job because I'm good at it, maybe better than anyone else, and because I enjoy it. I took your job because I believed I could do it and that at the money it was a good risk. I still believe that, but even if I didn't I would not – as you put it – turn tail because that way a mercenary very quickly runs out of clients. Like the Hive people, I too believe in the future: mine, and I value my reputation too highly to risk losing it in a tinpot little war like this one.

"You want to come with me? You want to ride a bomb into battle, against an adversary whose capabilities we can only guess? With instructions to limit the attack because the sods on the ground fancy the other ship as a souvenir? It's twenty years or more since you were in a space battle, Chaucer. Have you any idea what kind of armaments and tactics to expect? We use devices that will turn you white. Do you even know your emission tolerances after so long? Mine, you will not be surprised to learn, are high.

"I don't need your help, Chancellor, I don't need your company, and I don't want you crawling around my deck looking for somewhere to be sick. But I will take you, if that's what you require, on the clear understanding that if you get in my way I will move you." The pitch of his voice and the fire in his eyes implied greater violence than the words.

Again, as in the Council chamber, the gaze of the two men met with a percussion that seemed to reverberate round the small room and should have registered on the oscilloscopes. Between them they seemed to hold time still. There was no sound, no movement; even the green blip on the scanner seemed to pause. The confrontation was more overt, less mannerly than before. Again Chaucer ended it. Again Paul was left plunging in a mental turbulence of relief, frustration, obscure humiliation and the acute awareness of having won nothing. He would have been happier for knowing the worry he was causing his opponent.

The Chancellor backed off with serpentine slickness. "I accept your conditions," he said; too easily, Paul did not believe a word of it, had he meant it he would have grudged it like blood, but Paul was at a loss to know what Chaucer expected to gain by chicanery now. Still he would sooner have gone into battle with a loose snake on "Gyr's" flight-deck than with the lord Chaucer in the right-hand seat.

But his choice in the matter was limited. Faced with obduracy on the part of the Mithraian, all he could really do was refuse to fly, and if he did that he had no illusions about his chances either of leaving Mithras or enjoying a long stay upon it. Besides – and this was the point Chaucer failed to appreciate – he did not want to miss the battle. He had come a long way for it, done a lot of work on it and expected to be paid a lot of money for it; but more than all this his blood was up. He was a fighting man by breeding, training, talent and every natural instinct, and he would have flown "Gyr" with both Chaucer and the snake on his back rather than be disappointed now. He needed this engagement like an addict needs a fix. Shah said he was immoral. Paul made the scorpion's reply, conveniently forgetting that the scorpion drowned.

Unhappy as he was, then, there was nothing for him to think about. "Damn you, come on," he growled, shouldering past Chaucer to the door. From the corridor all the way to the parked, glistening shuttle he kept up a steady jog, but though Chaucer was breathing more heavily than he at the end Paul was denied the satisfaction of either seeing him fall behind or feeling him hurt to keep up.

Air and Darkness

Chapter One

They lost the drone. For some time as they stole deeper into the grey world – and their eyes adjusting to its spectrum began to recognise subtleties of shade and tone: smoky blue smudges in the bark, a blush of rose along a sappy stem, tiny bright stars of white and yellow flowers peeking from the mossy forest floor, and the myriad variations on the green theme which gained in intensity what, sun-starved, they lost in brilliance – Shah believed she had the silent figure in view; or if not that exactly, that she knew how far ahead he moved and where he travelled. She could not dog him with her mind, for all the vibrant coruscating images that flooded in when she opened the sluices. With her embryonic understanding of just what this great imprecise intellect was, she was not surprised that trying to track a solitary Drone through it proved no more feasible than trailing a firefly across a field of meteors. Still she thought she knew where he was, until she got there and there was no sign of him. She looked at Michal and Michal looked at her, and each knew as surely as if it had been written large in fluorescent letters that the one had no more idea where they were than the other.

Michal coped with the disaster with admirable fortitude. Being lost was just another addition to the long list of terrors a man should expect who ventured into a forest. Already beyond panic, he greeted the development as a martyr, with soulful resignation.

Curiously – or perhaps not so, given that Michal had long passed his credulity threshold while this was hers – Shah was more distressed than the Mithraian. She never got lost. Wherever she wandered there were minds she could tap into to learn where she was and how to get where she was going. She had only ever been lost once, and that was in the ice-and-fire depths of a man's psyche: Paul's, more expansive, more complex and contradictory, cleverer, angrier and lonelier than anything she had encountered in twenty years' mind-hopping. Now, her perception useless in this overwhelming confusion of perceptions, she was lost again – dazzled, deafened, her mental compass spinning. "Stop it," she gritted.

Michal, his alarm circuits almost exhausted, summoned up the last rather weary dregs in response to the sight of Shah turning slowly on her heels, then quicker, in the terrible grey-green place, crying out to no-one he could see, "Stop it – stop it – I'm drowning – STOP IT!" her voice rising at the last to a wail.

"Shah!" He caught her arms and shook her, and pulling her to him folded her against his chest, absorbing the shudders of her long body with his own. She clung to him like a frightened child. Slowly the tremors ceased.

She mumbled into his shoulder, "It's stopped."

"What has?" There was concern, and more, in Michal's scratched and dirty face.

Shah did not look at his face. "Oh God, how am I going to tell you? Michal, there's something in the forest – no. No. The forest – the forest itself – was talking to me. Not out loud; in my head. I'm a telepath. This forest is intelligent, and communicative, and telepathic. It was hammering my brain in its need to communicate. It's stopped now."

Michal said nothing. Nothing at all suitable came to mind. He did not know if he was mad or if she was, and though it seemed likely that one of them was it did not seem all that important which. He went on holding her, only glad that he had finally come in useful.

At length Shah raised her head from Michal's breast and said quietly, "He's over there."

The Drone was sitting under a great silver-grey tree, gnarled with age, sparsely peppered with turning leaves. Many of its leaves were already fallen among its knotty spreading roots, arthritic as its branches, where they formed a thick palliasse for the squatting

Drone. The stocky creature, perfectly camouflaged, sat quite still, and the dead leaves made no sound. The Drone's round eyes, half hooded, studied the man and woman knowingly. He was chewing thoughtfully on a dry twig.

Shah straightened out of Michal's arms. Still holding his hand, she took a few soft steps towards the small impassive figure. "May we speak with you?"

Michal tugged her hand and whispered, "They cannot talk."

"They can talk to me," said Shah. "Can't you?"

The Drone inclined his grizzled head. He took the stick from his mouth and with it indicated the leaf carpet beside him, under the tree. Shah folded gracefully cross-legged before him. The leaves whispered around her. Michal, reluctantly and more awkwardly, sat down beside her, eyeing the forest creature with disfavour and distrust.

"We are not a tolerant entity," said the Drone; or something very like it, though the words he used and the sense he made were often at variance and his sentence structuring suffered from a confusion or possibly a deliberate blurring between the singular and plural when he spoke in the first person. It soon became clear that the grey man was not so much speaking as providing a means of communication for another: another whom Shah associated, intuitively or fortuitously but anyway correctly, with the massive consciousness of which she was already aware. What that consciousness was also became clear, as the Drone proceeded.

"We are not a tolerant entity," but we were prepared to tolerate the people of the ship. They were few, compared with us, and they lacked the means to become many. They were crippled and had nowhere else to go, and once here they could not leave. We would have preferred for them to have been cast away elsewhere, but we were not blind to the probability of their feeling the same way. We were prepared to co-exist for the remainder of their lifetimes, which is not a great span measured as we measure it.

"They cut into the forest. They hacked and laid waste and burned, and let in the sun. This caused us pain, and anger waxed in us.

But the people needed a place of dwelling, and if they could not live in the forest it was not perhaps unreasonable for them to make a clearing. The forest is great. We endured their small vandalism. Then they dug into the earth. This was to make bricks for their dwelling. We endured. They dug deeper, for oil to power their Hive. They needed power. We endured. They dug fields and tanks, for food. Still we endured.

"They they took the crystals. This made us very angry. The crystals could not shelter them, feed them, warm them or give them light. They have no possible use or function – they are merely a by-product of our planet's natural chemistry. As such they are a part of that unity which all the elements of our world compose. The people had no good reason to take them. We began to hate them for their rapacity.

"We endured still while they contented themselves with those crystals they took from the workings in the small world of their clearing. But when they came into the forest, and toppled trees that had been centuries in the growing to steal the crystals nestling under their roots, we could tolerate no more. The forest exacted a vengeance. Those who came paid back to the earth something of the richness they had wrung from it. After that the people stayed out of the forest."

Michal said, "Shah, this is pointless – that thing could not talk if it wanted to. Let us go home."

Before she had time to register surprise at his words, Shah felt the surge of animosity focusing on him: not so much from the Drone, who remained impassive, as from the trees and the mossy living carpet and beneath that the ground itself. There was nothing to see, but Michal caught his breath and bent his head into his hands and rolled slowly onto his side, and a little whimper escaped him.

Shah said sharply, "Leave him be."

The Drone said mildly, "He is one of the Hive people. He has no business here." He was watching Michal twitch with gentle satisfaction.

"I'm here because you asked me to come," rapped Shah, "and

he is here because I asked him to come, and if you want any favours from me you will keep your hands, fronds and minds off my friends."

The squatting Drone sounded amused, though his eyes were as flat as ever. "You surely do not think you can fight us for him?"

"I can not only fight you but beat you, unless you are prepared to sacrifice whatever usefulness you believe I have. You didn't summon me here only to discuss your grievances. Contend with me, then, at your peril."

From the quality of the grey-green silence Shah judged she had succeeded in startling the Drone, or rather the consciousness which animated it. Its amazement, however, could be no more than a pale shadow of her own. Sometimes, she thought with a sense of wonder, I do things that make Paul's activities look like a textbook on discretion.

The Drone said, pettishly, "Have him." The tight knot of Michal's body slackened suddenly and he rolled onto his face, moaning.

Shah ignored him, thinking it best. She said, "I was about to enquire what you did to them. I no longer feel the need to ask."

"We are not a tolerant entity," the Drone said again. The word 'entity' seemed increasingly to indicate a community, a consensus, a totality. "We expect to see debts repaid and reparations made by despoilers. As the air absorbs those that invade it, so the forest consumes those who trespass here. We waste very little."

"I'm sure you're an example to us all," Shah said coldly.

"This is our world," replied the Drone. "It suits us; it has no need to suit others. Those who cannot cope with its nature should leave; those who cannot leave must learn to cope."

"I can cope," said Shah. "I can also leave. So you're going to have to come to terms with me."

"You are angry. Over them?" The Drone regarded Michal as Shah might regard a slug.

"I don't think a lot of the people of the Hive. They're greedy, lazy, cruel and decadent, and taken as a whole – there are notable exceptions – they haven't the initiative to come in out of the rain. But even they appear winsome by comparison with blood-thirsty trees. You'll never know how lucky you were to have the Hive people land here, with their shiftless get-rich-quick-or-don't-bother philosophy. The galaxy is teeming with peoples who would have turned your planet into a farm by now, and marshalled your damned trees into hedgerows."

"Is it also," asked the Drone, "teeming with telepaths?"

Shah took a hold on her temper. "No, I don't believe so."

"Then we have been doubly lucky."

"What do you want with me?"

Shah was conscious of being surveyed, inspected, from more angles than were available to the unmoving Drone. The response was long in coming. "The – thing – was right. We cannot talk. We are not talking now. See: our mouth moves only upon the twig. No sounds come, none that he can hear. We speak only upon the ether. He speaks only on the audio frequencies. You have access to both.

"In the long past these you call Drones were as he is now. They evolved as he did, communicated as he does, formed cultures not dissimilar to his. They passed their days in comparable, though hopefully more profitable, ways for a million years. Then we out-evolved him. We became like you. Our minds learned to speak soundlessly. We found truth and beauty and great comfort in that community of thoughts, and over generations we lost the desire and thereafter the means to speak aloud. We passed into the great silence, that lasted across this world – uninterrupted except by the murmur of the leaves – until the ship came."

"Are there no birds, no insects?" asked Shah: she no longer knew if she spoke words or thought them.

"Neither. There were both, but we destroyed them in our growing. It was not intentional. It happened before we knew it, and only afterwards did we understand how. We achieved the zenith of our physical evolution at the expense of all other life. Only the trees endured. So we made our communion with the trees.

"Now our evolution is taking us beyond you too. You look at this small, shambling, silent creature, brown and grey like the deep forest, slow and unresponsive, without grace or greatness, and you take him for an evolutionary cast-off, a withering branch, his line either aborted in its destiny or over-peaked and degenerating. In way you are right. His physical form is degenerative. Its usefulness is coming to an end. His grandchildren's children, or their children, will have no bodies at all.

"We are in a process of transition. Soon – as we measure time – no tangible fabric will stand between these people, their thoughts and the totality of their environment. Wholly psychic beings, unrestricted by weak and cumbrous bodies, they will live forever, grow immeasurably great, learn unknowable things. The world will be their body and their spirit will inhabit the trees. Where there is now communion there will be unity. The people of Mithras – the real, original, enduring and undying people of Mithras – are in the process of becoming their own god."

Shah's skin crawled and her scalp pricked eerily. She whispered, "There would be no people."

"That is another way of putting it."

"This is what you want?"

The Drone seemed to laugh, although no ripples disturbed his bland face. "Our desires are hardly a prime consideration when evolution is determining its goal. For be assured, this is the fate of nations: ours, yours, his, any that survives the dangers of its own angry adolescence must come at last to this maturity. Where else is there to go?

"But since you ask the question, then yes: the prospect is pleasing to us. We have been in the world a very long time. We know it intimately. It is a world characterised by conflict. In our youth we thrived on conflict, conquering and relishing both battle and victory. Later the charms of war palled. We strove for equilibrium, for a world in balance, without violence or change. But the nature of the physical world is to change, to develop, and the universal laws of progression would not stand still because we of Mithras had reached where we wanted to be. We are weary of contention – even the small daily contentions necessary to life: obtaining food, drinking, selecting mates in order to reproduce our kind. We are tired of life as you know it. We crave peace: not the defeat which is death but the continuing peace of stasis. We are ready to step aside onto that parallel plane where the demands of physical existence have no place and only the freed mind may face the centuries with serenity."

"But," ventured Shah, "won't you be bored?"

"Oh no," said the Drone with conviction. "Oh dear me no."

Michal was back in the land of the living. With the heightened consciousness that came of talking with the Drone, even without probing Shah was aware of the hurt in him. His pain and his fear grieved her, because she held herself responsible more than either the Drone or the forest. The safety of the Hive was both tenuous and transitory, but it held good for as long as the illusion of it lasted. Shah had pricked that bubble, and Michal would never know security again. He knelt hollow-eyed, awash with despair. Shah put out her arm and drew him to her. He sat against her, not looking at her, mute, like an injured sheepdog. His spirit had been the only gentleness on a harsh world full of egotists, and she had damaged it; and if she had destroyed it the memory of that lost trust would be as a haunting to her. Soon now, she promised a trifle absently, she would take him out of this baleful wood and see what could be done about repairing him; but first there was this other matter to resolve.

"I still don't understand what role you expect me to play."

"Recorder," said the Drone. "We wish some record of our sojourn on this world, and our continuing association with it, to pass out to the stars. We do not know if we are the first people to achieve this translation. In the nature of things it seems unlikely; and yet we are an ancient race, we know of none older, and nothing we have heard suggests that others have reached this ultimate haven first. The galaxies should know that Mithras was once the home of men and will soon be the nucleus of a unified cosmic intellect. Mithras will be the first sentient world."

"But what do you want me to *do*?" cried Shah.

"You need do nothing more," said the Drone. "You have listened. You will remember. While you live, wherever you go you will seed the memory of Mithras, whether you would or not. You are our heir, custodian of our history. The key to the mystery of life lies in your hands. You may hold it or bestow it elsewhere, but you cannot return it. The burden of knowledge is yours. Our task is done."

The Drone was gone. Shah supposed dully that he must have got up and walked away but – introspectively brooding, wrestling with the onus Mithras had tricked her into accepting, feeling the enormity of the heritage weighing on her mind and spirit and bones, angry and sour with feelings of having been deceived and betrayed although in fact neither deceit nor betrayal had been employed – she did not notice. She noticed very little for quite some time. Then, gradually, reason and good faith began to reassert themselves. If it was true that she had been used, at least she had not been abused. The knowledge lodged with her, however unwelcome in its concentrated form, was fascinating, even wondrous, and might conceivably do someone some good some day. If she did not know what to do with it now, it was probably also the case that there was nothing she could do with it now, least of all give it back. Like a cure for piles, she thought with a sudden glint of humour, the day would come when it would seem very important indeed, but in the meantime the whole strange portentous saga could be safely relegated to a mental bottom drawer. The weight lifted.

About that time she realised that the deafening psychic clamour of the silent forest that had yielded only to the Drone had returned but in a transmuted form, mayhem shrunk to a friendly murmur; and that Michal was still on his knees beside her like a penitent. She tapped the back of his hand with a grimy forefinger. "If you stay like that much longer your legs will go to sleep."

Michal breathed an audible sigh. He stood up and looked round at the grey-green jungle. He looked up at the streamers of pale light pricking through the high leaf canopy. His eyes were blank, almost as flat as the Drone's. There was no image of his thoughts in them. He offered his hand.

Shah took it and let him draw her up. "I don't suppose you understood much of what was going on there."

He looked blankly at her. "There was nothing to understand. You and that thing stared at each other. I asked you to come away. Something hurt me. I do not know if it was you or it. I doubt if it matters. You are part of this, are you not?" Distress was creeping visibly into his eyes and audibly into his voice. His hand waved unsteadily. "This damned forest has strangled and bled us for fifteen years. Now when we finally get help we find even our rescuers prefer the forest! God knows, Shah, I have few enough illusions about my people – but can we possibly be worse than lethal trees and devious snake-eyed little torturers? If even Mithras is too good for us, where shall we find rest?"

Tears shone in Shah's lustrous almond eyes. His plea flayed her soul. "Oh Michal, I wouldn't hurt you for worlds! I'm not siding with the forest, only listening to it. You can't imagine what's going on here, and they can't tell you – only me. But being able to speak on their frequency doesn't make me one of them. Some people hear a wider range of sounds than others, but hearing like a dog doesn't make you a dog."

"What is a dog?" asked Michal, without curiosity.

"I'll tell you," promised Shah. "I will tell you, everything we said, though I don't know how much you'll understand. I don't know if I really understand it myself. Paul will know." The memory of his terse, incisive intellect cut through the fog of her woolly thoughts like a beacon and she warmed to it. "Michal, we have to get out of here, back to the Hive. I have to talk to Paul."

"I want to go home," Michal said dully. Shah did not know if it were consent or protest or just an expression, as understated as the visible tip of an iceberg, of his new pain.

Shah took his arm, missing the thrill of pleasure that had greeted her earlier embraces. "Let's go home."

With the psychic activity of the forest diminished to a background hum, she was able to locate and follow that other susurration, harder-edged and more discordant, emanating from the Hive. They walked between the grey columns, silent on the soft ground, until the strengthening sun raised up the green thicket before their faces. Their eyes had adjusted to the subtle tones of the deep wood: the bright verdure of the thrusting, coiling hedge seemed to them livid to the point of vulgarity.

It offered them no hindrance. They passed through it as they had seen the Drone do. The brambles seemed to coil out of their way, the clutching thorns unzipping. Still Shah held onto Michal's hand as if both their lives depended on it.

Where the hedge yielded, abruptly and with a bad grace, to the clearing, Michal stopped, literally and metaphorically poised between two worlds. He stood quite still, looking out across the scoured earth.

Shah stopped beside him, searching his blank face anxiously. "What is it, Michal?"

He nodded at the Hive. "It has shrunk," he said. "And it is ugly."

Hurting for him, Shah pushed past to draw him into the sun. "Come on, let's see what they've all been up to. Look, there's the shuttle. Paul's inside: I can feel him. There's someone with him. And there's –"

It was Balrig, the foppish captain of Hornet Patrol, and he was standing close by a well-head installation and pointing at her. Michal jerked out of his lethargy fast enough to shout, "No!" and drag back on her hand, but as she spun, off-balance and bewildered, without warning her right breast exploded sending pain and shock like debris hurtling through her body.

She lurched against Michal, stunned dumb, her eyes stretched and glazing. She dimly felt his arms around her, vaguely heard his voice. She could not breathe. Darkness crowded in. The last thing she knew was a throaty roar in her ears that she at first took for the flood-tide of death, then correctly identified as the engines of the shuttle coughing into life as she coughed out of it; and the recognition, which struck her as wryly typical of Mithras, that she was going to die taking perhaps the most sensational revelation in the known cosmos with her, untold. She tried, in the last moment of awareness left to her, to pass the knowledge on to her companion; but it had taken an hour of synapse-to-synapse communication between her and a planet for her to acquire it, and if Michal could decipher her faint whispered words he could make nothing of them, and soon the whispering ceased.

Chapter Two

Afterwards Paul searched his memory with obsessional thoroughness for anything that hinted, even in retrospect, at the events occurring only a stone's throw away as he put the shuttle through its ground checks. The recognition that, seek as he might, there was nothing to find convinced him as nothing else could have done that his own lost perception was not sleeping, not maimed, but dead. If anything had survived the holocaust in his head he must have felt the pangs of Shah's agony then, and he felt nothing.

The shuttle mounted slowly until it was level with the top of the Hive. Then Paul vectored the thrust abruptly aft, and the little craft, its oiled planes catching the sun, shot forward like a racehorse from a starting-stall. It banked sharply round the conical apex – sending Amalthea's clawed hands clapping to her ears with a lack of aplomb that would have been ample reward could Paul have seen it – before settling into the curving climb that would take it up to "Gyr". The flight-path was devised to intercept "Gyr's" orbit while the disc of Mithras masked her from the pirate ship. Paul did not know how good the SAM's instrumentation was – possibly by now it was no more half-hearted than its armaments – but whatever there was of it would be focussed on the planet and its environs as soon as an image could be resolved. If the imaging was good they would already have seen "Gyr" and would know that the Hive had summoned aid, but Paul saw no reason to notify them that their approach was being monitored and a welcome prepared by displaying open activity around the battleship. By the time "Gyr" hove back into view the shuttle would be stowed and no change in status apparent. The small deceit might not fool them long, but every minute he could keep them guessing was ammunition in the psychology of combat.

He had forgotten Chaucer the moment the shuttle's console came to life under his touch, and he did not think of him again until the craft had coupled with the docking flanges and been drawn up into its bay in the midsection hold, the great silent doors shutting out the starlight. He felt the quake of their meeting as a shiver through the fabric of the black ship which awoke corresponding resonances along the nerves of his own skin. The tremor, final as a falling axe, put the seal on commitment. Paul switched on the infra-red.

Chaucer's face leapt into livid perspective beside him. The light was not flattering. The rosy flush along his cheeks and red glints in his eyes and beard were evocative of primaeval power: the Chancellor would have been worshipped as a devil on half a dozen worlds of Paul's acquaintance. He leaned forward into the red light, eagerly, and for a silly surrealist moment Paul half expected him to flash a smile rich in vampire incisors. Grinning to himself at the thought, he wriggled out of his seat and through the airlock. "I'd bid you welcome to my ship," he said, "but you might think I meant it."

"I would express my admiration," smiled Chaucer, looking round him, "but you might take it for covetousness."

For the purposes of selling her services "Gyr" was described as an interstellar battle-cruiser. That made her a big ship. She was a particularly big ship for two people to go rattling around in, but Paul – who had had her to himself often in the past – had never heard the emptiness echo as it did now with a stranger dogging his heels where Shah should have been.

In fact the accomodation on "Gyr" was not greatly out of proportion to the size of her complement. She had been designed and built for Paul, customised to the way he worked. Most of the bulk of the black ship was to do with her function and the nature of her voyages. Banks of armaments hedged her round with teeth. Her field of fire was virtually spherical, the batteries computer-governed and capable of as many operating patterns as the pilot cared to program. In a defensive watch-dog mode, she could direct a single burst from the most convenient muzzle to pick off any craft venturing within a buffer-zone defined by laser locaters. By contrast, the main cannon ranged across the bow and the leading edges of the manta wings could belt out enough sheer attacking force to disintegrate a good-sized asteroid.

Bomb-rooms ran through the spine of the ship, separated from the fury of the guns by double blast-doors and stores of less sensitive equipment: water-tanks and purifiers, deep-frozen provisions for voyages years in duration, workshops, a laboratory that doubled as a medical unit, and supplies of spare parts for every aspect of the ship that could conceivably go wrong. Paul had no idea what some of them were, although he had lived and breathed this ship since before her launch. He entertained the sneaking suspicion that some of the odder items did not belong to "Gyr" at all, and only hoped that nothing vital of his was touring the scenic far side of the universe in the bowels of the ship whose substitute insides he had brought to Mithras.

Centrally located at either end of the flight of bomb-rooms were the shield generators: a pair of them, each capable of sustaining the emission field which was "Gyr's" prime defence through any probable assault. In the improbable event of "Gyr" meeting a cruiser of equivalent firepower, the old irresistible force/immovable object paradox would be resolved, though Paul doubted if there would be any survivors to report the outcome.

The other main essentials of the ship were located in the wings to either side of the flight-deck: the ventilator, the main computer, the navigation system, the radio equipment. Failure in any of these areas meant failure of a mission and probable loss of the ship. Since there was little point in the crew surviving an assault if the life-support systems did not, the whole forward section of the ship was designed as one unit, to become its own lifeboat in the event of massive damage to the after-section. It was a fairly tenuous prospect of salvation for a crew heavily beset, but it was the only one. Disaster among the stars tended to be total.

Completing the outline of the ship, four great engines stepped out on sweeping brackets girdled the stern section. That segment of space immediately behind her was the only gap in the globe of "Gyr's" gunnery. It was not an omission. With four ion-drive engines pointed at them, no foreseeable enemy could hold together long enough to inflict damage. For all the cannon, lasers, torpedoes, missiles and exotic particle-rays in the catalogues of the interstellar arms merchants, nothing in space was more irresistibly lethal than the standard unit of power by which men crossed it. The fact was assiduously kept from the tourist classes who ventured abroad for pleasure and would have stayed at home had they known they rode Armageddon.

Chaucer's leonine head was turned with looking all ways at once as Paul conducted him through to the flight-deck. Any stubborn disappointment that had survived thus far vanished there. "Gyr's" control centre was massively impressive, and more rather than less so for the designer's obvious lack of interest in appearances. What impressed was the supreme unadorned efficiency of a layout of screens and instruments and terminals, in broad banks that filled all the horse-shoe wall and half the curved ceiling, and all of them focused on the pilot. Sitting there, mused Chaucer, with so much power and so much death at his finger-ends, a man must feel like a god. He stole a sidelong look at Paul, already bent over a screen and thumbing up figures, and wondered if that was how he felt: like a god for hire. He wondered how gods felt about losing their divinity.

Paul dropped into the driving-seat and became part of his ship. He said without looking up, "Find yourself somewhere to sit and don't interrupt me."

"I can help you, if you will let me."

Paul looked round at him, narrow-eyed. Then he nodded. "All right. Run those through the computer." It was the sheaf of calculations he had brought from the Hive. "I'll call it up for you."

The hairs over the crest of his head and others Chaucer was unaware of down his neck and back stood up like soldiers at the realisation that the words were literally meant. Paul talked to his ship. It disturbed something fundamental in Chaucer's view of the universe, in which machines were machines and intelligence was the prerogative of his people or those indistinguishable from them. The ability to communicate verbally was too close to intelligence for comfort, and he waited with his skin creeping to see if the computer would speak back. It did not. The eerie sensation subsided, but the unease did not. If "Gyr" was atuned to Paul's voice, suborning it might prove infinitely more difficult than he had anticipated.

No dark thoughts troubled Paul's mind. The Mithraian's assessment was correct: here he was a god in his own country – at home, confident, invulnerable. "Gyr" was his spiritual as well as actual power-base: all his strengths were rooted in her. He was not unconscious of the profound dangers that intermittently he faced with her. But he believed that she was probably the best fighting ship in the galaxy and that he was, taken all round, probably the best fighting man. If he also knew that no-one is more vulnerable than a man who believes implicitly in his own superiority, here in the heady miasma of the incense rising in his own temple he had forgotten. Arrogance is the weakness of the strong.

"Gyr's" instruments, better positioned and considerably more sophisticated than the al fresco devices in the Hive's tiny radio-room, picked up the approaching vessel as soon as she swung clear of the planetary disc. It was reasonable, or at least cautious, to assume that the pirates saw "Gyr" at the same time, but Paul doubted if they enjoyed an image as clear as that which now flashed up on his screen and made Chaucer start like a hound scenting quarry.

"That is them," he rapped, his diamond eyes kindling. "But something is amiss – they should not yet be within screen range."

Paul grinned, not kindly. "I told you, the art of warfare has moved on in the last twenty years. Intercept is where and when I indicated. Long before that you'll be able to count the rivets in her plates."

To all appearances, even on "Gyr's" screen, the vessel was identical to a myriad other semi-armed merchantmen trading the star-routes. A giant hold with crew quarters at the front and a single ion engine at the back, they looked like nothing so much as a fleet of lit cigars. The standard armaments included medium-range cannon, close-combat lasers, a radar confusion capability commonly if inexplicably called Window, and a shield generator notionally though not effectively comparable with "Gyr's". The SAM weapons system was devised as an answer to renegades and local thugs, not to battleships.

As to her non-standard armoury, Paul had only Chaucer's description of the earlier attacks. This time when she opened fire, computers tied in to "Gyr's" shields would plot every shell and swiftly draw up a profile of her fight characteristics. In the meantime Paul added twenty per cent to the estimates given him by Chaucer and fed those into the main computer as a working hypothesis.

Long ago, in Chaucer's vanished and little-regretted youth, on the small world that subsequently became the first colony of Amalthea's first empire, there was a craze for shooting electronic aliens out of an electronic sky at ten shots a chip. The machines appeared in drinking-docks and pleasure palaces and transit stations in every city of the developed globe, to the accompaniment of flashing lights and explosive sound-effects and the chink of money. They went by such unashamedly chauvinistic names as Zap-a-Wog, and the idea was to shoot the approaching aliens off the screen before they could land and invade. For five years the game enjoyed a vogue akin to mass addiction, so that every coin in the treasury had first been through eight Zap-a-Wogs. Then, as is the way with crazes, interest began to wane. Interest finally died beyond hope of resurrection when a fleet of ships arrived from a neighbouring star-system bearing real aliens with black claws and guns who colonised the little planet virtually without hindrance while most of the population was playing Spot-the-Clone. Amalthea soon stopped them playing games.

But when Chaucer turned from his frankly avaricious appraisal of "Gyr's" flight-deck to find her commander apparently engrossed in a game of Zap-a-Wog on the computer screen his mouth went dry, his hands balled into fists and his heart skipped a beat, turned over and sank. With what he considered commendable restraint in the circumstances he managed to choke out, "What are you *doing*?"

Paul looked up, distracted and scowling. "I told you, don't get in my way. I haven't so much time I can afford to waste it giving you a conducted tour." Then he seemed to see the real horror in Chaucer's seraphic face and he leaned back. "Look, don't you understand? We'll only get one chance at that corsair. If I get it wrong it's going to cost me – my ship will get hurt, maybe I'll get hurt, quite possibly I'll have to blow the ungodly out of the sky, and then I'll have to explain why to Amalthea. Thanks to your total lack of aptitude for self-defence, I don't know what armaments I have to contend with. I can guess, or I can wait and see. Or I can program every possibility I can think of into the computer and let it show me what the result would look like – so that when I try spiking his engine and suddenly find myself eating his flak I know he's got an Immelmann capability because I've seen it before, on this." He stroked patterns over the console, his strong fingers on the keys as unconsciously sensual as if the instrument were a woman's body, and the sketched image leapt and spat fire at him.

As Chaucer watched the little ship race through a whole war's worth of manoeuvres, the horror in his eyes yielded temporarily to fascination before slowly regaining the ascendancy. "You mean, that freighter can *do* all those things?"

Paul grinned wolfishly, relishing his alarm. "Not all at once, I hope."

The bourgeois, complacent society of the little lost world submitted immediately and totally to the invader's rule. But it quickly became apparent to Amalthea that taking a planet and ruling it as a colony were two different skills, and though she had plenty of warriors few knew the art of administration. Those who did, did well; and none did better than Chaucer, with his intelligence, his ambition, his capacity for work and his talent for manipulation that amounted almost to genius. After that, wherever Amalthea looked to extend her empire Chaucer went with her. He had been with her longer than any other member of her entourage, and she still frightened the life out of him. But she had never had cause to regret advancing him and, other than that he would not have chosen to be stranded on Mithras, Chaucer regretted nothing either.

Only he thought he might just regret, just fleetingly, what he was about to do here. It was not that he liked Paul – who could? – but that he, like Amalthea, recognised talent when he saw it and was sorry to see it wasted. But he was resigned, knowing that even on a chain a tiger makes a perilous pet. He said, "'Gyr': what does it mean?"

"Hm?" Paul straightened out of his concentrated hunch over the battle-screen and stretched, cat-like. He checked the time. There was a little of it still to kill and not much more he could do. He had a sudden craving for coffee. "Oh – it's a hunting bird. They fly them after game in the ice deserts on the planet where she was built."

"Is that where you were born?"

Paul eyed him wickedly and said with disconcerting candour, "I wasn't born, Chaucer – I was made. Coffee?"

Chaucer nodded, bemused, understanding the one precept about as well as the other.

Most of his adult life Paul had been alone. It had brought out unexpected strains of domesticity in him. Unless pressed by absolute necessity he never went more than twenty-four hours without cooking a proper meal, and he never left the washing-up. He was infinitely better in the galley than Shah, who was vague in approach and untidy in application. But she had brought a little gaiety into the functional place when she provisioned for the trip at a travelling Tawdry Fair, as a result of which the mugs which presently Paul brought, steaming, onto the flight-deck bore the legends "Celibacy leaves a lot to be desired" and "Apathy rules OK but who cares?" After a moment's consideration he gave Chaucer "Apathy".

Chaucer drank and coughed. "That is disgusting."

Paul looked surprised. "Is it?" He drank. "Well, you wouldn't want me nodding off in the middle of things. You can toast my success in something more to your taste when we get back to the Hive."

Chaucer kept on at the coffee like a man worrying a sore tooth. He nodded a general gesture around the bridge. "Who did you steal her from?"

"Shah?"

"'Gyr'."

"I didn't steal her." His tone was flat, but the astute Chaucer could hear in his voice a pride of which Paul was quite possibly unaware. "I earned her. With ten years' work, and a lot of sweat, and a lot of pain. It was in the nature of a wager. The people I did the work for gambled I wouldn't live long enough to collect."

"You did. Others did not?"

"I don't even know how many." It might have been a boast, but Chaucer believed the bleakness in his eyes. He had seen such a look before, years ago, in the deep crypt of an aesthete's temple renowned through half the empire for the beauty and sensitivity of its ancient paintings. Chaucer had asked the meaning of one of the figures. The aesthete guiding him had replied, "That is Lucifer, remembering the sun." Paul had the eyes of a devil sick of sin.

"So they gave you this ship."

The mercenary grinned, without much humour. Chaucer, who did not labour beneath an overly tender conscience, was aware that he smiled at all the wrong things. "I managed to persuade them that they should. Come on," he said then, easing back into his seat, "let's get this war on the road."

Chapter Three

The great engines awoke like angry mountains. The throb of their rage shook the ship; the roar of their fury was an untenable agony against Chaucer's eardrums; for only a brief moment. Then the accelerating battleship left behind all her own sound, taking with her only a deep subliminal thrum in her plates that those aboard could forget about for hours at a time but never quite completely.

In the same way it was possible to fly a ship through deep space, and for the routine of flying her to become so automatic and the sight of the lazy swimming stars so commonplace that the wonder of the thing was lost under the sheer weight of the familiarity. Whole treks were shrunk to simulator scale. But if a man left the comfort of his padded chair and walked over to the wall, and laid his hands against it, the deep thrumming in his fingertips would remind him that infinity began only four alloy inches away, and then the awesome majesty of all the cosmic miles came crowding in – as profoundly crushing to the psyche as if the endless vacuum itself had poured in through an actual hole in the fabric of the craft, fragile as gossamer in the context of the silent shimmering void.

Many men found they could not endure the burden of loneliness awaiting the children of suns in the dark wastes between the stars. Others, a few, found a curious heady stimulation in the very disparity of scale between man and the universe. They were known, in the places where space crew congregate – the docks and transit stations and cargo depots corporately known by the ancient and anachronistic name The Waterfront – as Users; the implication of the label, which was bestowed with a kind of grudging admiration mixed with mistrust by the ordinary crewmen who could best deal with space by ignoring it for a large part of the time, being that the void consumed like that was addictive and that those who courted it conquered nothing, only succumbed to its lethal magnetism.

Paul loved deep space with the great, quiet passion of a man for his inheritance. In terms of mere time he was a novice – he knew men who had been eighty years in space, their lives stretched by decades of chasing the speed of light in the days before the star-drive, their old bodies now so adapted to the life that their bones broke when they ventured ashore – but he had not come virgin to the void. His first flight had been as a home-coming, things he had never known striking him with forceful familiarity. In dark and sparkling space he found an expanded version, unlimited by horizons, of the emotional peace and freedom he had found and cherished in the harsh, unremitting, pristine wastes of the ice desert of his native planet. There was cleansing in so much distance and so little humanity. In his sourer moods he thought of mankind as the great pollutant, insidiously spreading, irresistibly poisoning: a colonial corruption, a cancer. He was not immune to the feeling of isolation that afflicted other men, but he preferred solitude where there were no people to loneliness among people who feared him as he despised them. Also, there was great beauty and order in the stars which he did not see reflected in those who inhabited the little busy worlds. This was less their fault than his, but it was an inescapable facet of his conditioning that he had been brought up to understand machines, including celestial mechanics, more clearly than people.

But now he was in his element. Doing the task he had been bred for – fusing human insights and inspirations with inhuman reactions, wielding the product with a computer-like logic and the conscience of a submachine-gun – Paul was as much a weapon of war as his ship. The secret men who made both had wrestled for an age with the problem of creating the universal soldier, the intellect of a man safe in the steel body of a robot. Only with Paul did they recognise the potential for progress in the opposite direction.

They went a long way with Paul, but perhaps not far enough. They left too much of the man inside his brain: no weakness, but too much will; no fear, but too much anger; no compassion, but too much hatred. With telepathy too he was more than invincible – he was uncontrollable. So they took away his perception. But they could not destroy his memory of godhood, and memory and hatred and anger and will were enough to sustain him until he could trap them into giving him his freedom and his ship. His business was still, crudely speaking, death; but then it was never the business he objected to, only the people he worked for. Facing death – his own, someone else's, no matter – with only his lightning hands and his quicker wits between the one and the other was Paul's idea of living, so that by contrast the spaces between confrontations seemed trivial, nondescript, little more than padding inserted to stretch his span out to a respectable length. He could have done happily without them, but not without his personal fix of space and cold death. Yet still he deluded himself, as users will, that he had command of his habit.

"Gyr" made one swing round the back of Mithras, a lengthening ellipse that piled on the acceleration until the four great engines seemed in imminent danger of overtaking the ship they drove, or pushing the cockpit seats clean through the bodies of the men occupying them; then she leapt out clear of the disc and began her swift, avid consumption of the miles between her and her quarry.

The men of the "Quasar Griffin" were not expecting problems. They believed they had already had, and dealt with, all the trouble Amalthea could throw at them. They were aware, perhaps uncomfortably aware, that they were traversing what might be described as Mithraian airspace, but knowing what they now did about Amalthea, including the fact that she was grounded, they saw no reason for particular concern.

Welland, the navigator, first saw the black ship in transit across the bright green disc. He blinked and she was gone. Part of the reason for this was her trajectory, which was a fine chord rather than a diameter, but mostly it was pure speed that got her out of the spot-light and safe into the inky maze before anyone on "Griffin" had a fix on her and before most of them knew she was there.

All Welland's common-sense told him that the fleeting silhouette had been an illusion, a trick of the eyes or a trick of the skies, that a spaceship climbing from Mithras was an impossibility. But all his instincts, which after twelve years in this job were well developed, told him that danger threatened and all his training was geared to optimum safety even at the cost of wasted time and effort. So he reported the possible sighting, and Meredith, the captain, instigated the recommended searches even though he too knew that an attack from the planet was out of the question.

"Griffin's" scanners were uninhibited by preconceptions and so found the impossible craft, climbing impossibly fast towards an encounter appallingly soon. The crew of the SAM stared horror-stricken at the projection. Then Meredith snarled, "That madwoman's got hold of a battleship!" and, fumble-fingered from haste and lack of practice, keyed in the shields.

"You want to fight or run?" asked Welland laconically.

"Are you kidding?" glowered the captain. "That's a bloody bastard cruiser!"

"Evasion course set and running," reported Welland.

"Cannon armed and operational, lasers armed and waiting," came the terse voice of the gunner, Van Tauber.

"Sod the cannon," swore Meredith, "I want shields and speed, and anyone with no function in either department can damn well pray."

"We can't outrun her," Welland said, lugubriously shaking his shaggy head.

"In space anything is possible," said Meredith, anxiously watching the screen and chewing his lip. "For example, she might blow up. This is not as improbable as it sounds, given what we know of the Mithras atmosphere. Or she might fire a pile, or lose her gyros, or the crew might be smitten with a sudden blindness or madness or leprosy. These are admittedly less likely interventions, but the longer we delay confrontation the better the chance that something will come up. Since our position could hardly be worse, any eventuality must be to our advantage. Christ, look at that bugger move!"

The "Quasar Griffin" responded to the approach of the alien craft by jinking violently onto a new heading. The crew, all of whom had by now congregated on the flight-deck, leaned automatically into the curve. When they had straightened up again Pieter Van Tauber observed grudgingly, "That's a lovely looking ship she's got hold of."

Meredith turned on him an eye cold with disfavour. His words dripped scorn. "That is *not* a lovely looking ship, young Pieter. If that was *our* ship, it would be lovely looking. If it were somebody else's ship hastening to our aid, it would look positively gorgeous. If it carried the admittedly rather tasteless insignia of the AKW Star Patrol, to which I pay an exorbitant amount of tax in view of the fact that its craft are seldom seen more than an afternoon's flying time from Big Molly's brothel on Lygros, I would not hear a word spoken against it.

"But since it is Amalthea's ship, young Pieter, and it is bearing up on us at a truly prodigious rate, and it is bristling with things that crack and spit fire and blow your arms and legs off, and all I have to meet it with is a length of drain-pipe powered by an outboard motor and protected by a shield generator salvaged off Noah's Ark – whose efficacy is such that we might actually be safer standing behind sheets of brown paper – then no, young Pieter, that is *not* a lovely looking ship, it's the ugliest, nastiest, meanest-looking bastard I've seen since the wife's father was bitten by a snake and the snake died."

Meredith's crew tittered appreciatively. They were men facing death in a vacuum, and they were able to raise a chuckle to a bit of corny rhetoric because the alternative was bursting into tears, and if they were not particularly brave men they were certainly not cowards. They shared close confines for months at a time, many of them had been friends for years, and all were bound in a web of mutual respect. Welland was treasured for his stoical humour, Van Tauber for his fierce loyalty, Hillaby for the deep caring behind his irascible tongue, so that everyone on "Griffin" was in his debt for devoted nursing during illness although his own constitution was so far from robust that the only way he could get into space at all was as a cook.

But none was more respected than Meredith, whose lack of brilliance (though not of competence) as a pilot in no way detracted from his genius as a leader of men. The Quasar Company which had employed him for twenty-two years, twelve of them as a commander, noted in his file that their senior captain ran his ship without protocol, without an officer/crew structure, without orders (only "suggestions", "earnest suggestions" and "fairly bloody strenuous suggestions") and, to a degree unprecedented in the haulage business, which was slow and unglamorous and plagued by in-fighting, without rancour. Meredith very seldom lost a cargo and almost never lost a man. A patient enquirer could have combed the galaxy without finding a person more directly opposite in every particular to Paul, yet Meredith was as impressive in his own way at his own job and he had more friends.

And his friends on the "Quasar Griffin" had confidence that, if there was a way of getting out of this situation alive, Meredith would find it – he had, after all, rescued the ship from Amalthea the previous season when she lured them to Mithras with a phoney distress signal – and that, if there was not, he would lead them as well into death as he had through their strange, often tedious, communal life.

Though the flight-deck was considerably larger, if less marvellously appointed, than "Gyr's", nineteen men packing round the screen filled, it to capacity. The air as well as the atmosphere grew thicker. The bat-shaped black ship, beautiful as Van Tauber said in the graceful economy of her lines and the purposeful thrust of her ascent, swelled perceptibly in the perspex as she ate the intervening miles.

The silence grew harder and more brittle until it broke. "For God's sake," wrung out Van Tauber, "can't I at least get in a couple of blasts from the cannon before she blows us out of the sky?"

"Gently, Pieter," murmured Meredith. "No, I don't want to start the shooting. That's a contest we can't possibly win – if we take her on we'll end up in fifteen different constellations. Perhaps if we don't fire she'll be reluctant to: it's the ship she wants, after all, at least it was before, so she won't want big holes in it. Still, there is one action we probably ought to take."

He thumbed down the communicator switches, opening a broad band of channels. "This is the 'Quasar Griffin' calling Amalthea of Mithras; 'Quasar Griffin' calling Amalthea of Mithras; come in, please."

Paul was surprised at the development, perhaps disproportionately so. It was not unknown for doomed men to try to bargain with Fate; still, it seemed somehow improbable that such communication should be couched in the formal language of the wireless operator's handbook. He reached for his switches. Chaucer's soft, heavy hand fell on his.

"I'll talk to them."

Paul twisted his head slowly and spoke with exaggerated patience. "Chaucer. Until I have this job wrapped up, mopped up and delivered with little bows on it, you will not even talk to me." His dark eyes, golden-aureoled, held the Chancellor unwinkingly until Chaucer removed his hand. Then he replied.

"'Quasar Griffin', this is the battle-cruiser 'Gyr'. I am equipped and prepared to reduce your vessel to a cloud of swarf and protein globules three miles across. Alternatively, I will accept your unconditional surrender. What I am not going to do is discuss any compromise between those options."

Meredith said, "Isn't it rather early to be talking about unconditional surrender?"

"Not really," said Paul. "Gyr" leapt to the cough of her main cannon. Flak stitched the eternal night with lines of brilliance. Where the bright seams converged a length ahead of "Griffin" they created an explosive eddy from which waves of force burgeoned outward, invisible except for their effect on the hapless merchantmen. "Griffin" reared on her tail like a startled horse as the shock waves broke under her nose and screwed through three parts of a circle before the stabilisers regained control.

Bruised and winded men picked themselves off the walls of the "Quasar Griffin". One man slid down unconscious, blood trickling from his temple. Hillaby caught him before he hit the floor and, grumbling, whisked him off to his bunk.

Meredith turned from the console – he and Welland alone had ridden the wave without upset, wedged safely in the left- and right-hand seats – and looked gravely round his crew. "I think it's time everybody strapped in: duty-watch in here, the rest of you in the mess. Don't worry about missing anything: if we win you'll be the first to know. Also if we lose."

He swung back to the speaker. "All right, 'Gyr', we acknowledge your superior fire-power. There's no need to labour the point. It was never actually at issue. These overgrown beer-cans were armed against native outriggers, not bloody destroyers."

"What is your arsenal?"

Meredith snorted. "Oh come on, now. It may not be spectacular but it's all the defence we have – you can't expect us to give it to you on a plate."

"If you choose to surrender."

"You'd have to persuade us we had something to gain."

"I thought I already had."

"'Gyr'," said Meredith grimly, "I do not doubt that you can demolish my ship with minimal difficulty and effort. If you do so my crew will die, but they will die quickly and cleanly and not at the hands of a gorgon with a grudge. We do not intend to engage you, that would be fatuous. But while I have power and steerage I will neither stop this ship nor turn her round. If you want 'Griffin' you'll have to punch holes in her, and much good she'll do you then."

Paul made a small wry grimace at the small silver grid which brought Meredith's voice into his ship. If asked he might have admitted to being mildly impressed, but probably not. "Oh well," he remarked to Chaucer, "I'll shake them up a bit, see what they say then."

There were weapons in "Gyr's" armoury that the men of the "Quasar Griffin" had only heard of, and some more precocious than that. Some of the bursts and poundings that rattled "Griffin's" hull Pieter Van Tauber could identify approximately from the characteristics listed in the manufacturers' specifications – not that he ever persuaded the Quasar Company to invest in the like of sound missiles or alternating field-beams. He once nearly got a charged particle lance, but the company changed its mind at the last minute and bought a new carpet for the head office instead.

Van Tauber, who like all experts was something of a fanatic, managed to glean a certain pleasure from finally seeing the supreme technology of war, long coveted, in action even from the sinister side; and his watch companions managed to find room in their fearful hearts for a mounting irritation at his frequent oddly conceived observations of the "Ah yes – scorch bombs – I said we should have had some of those" variety as the belaboured ship ricocheted from blast to blast along the crests of force-waves like an inexpert surfer.

Paul too was growing tetchy. He was not enjoying this as much as he had expected to. Without risk there was no satisfaction, and if the privateer refused to face him there was no risk. There was no skill involved in shot-peppering a sitting duck. The "Griffin" was not even making a good job of running away. Her only defence was obstinacy.

"Why don't they fight?" he snarled. "They must have something worth throwing at us. You can't make a living as a pirate on SAM weaponry."

"They were not noticeably reticent about turning their guns on people on the ground," Chaucer said, tight-lipped.

"I suppose they reckon 'Gyr's' a whole new ball-game. Can't blame them for that." His lip curled reflectively. Disappointment soured his eyes. "Still, if they won't stop and they won't fight, we're left with just two options – destroy them or let them go. I doubt I need ask your preference."

Chaucer leaned over the arm of his chair, his big body animated. "No. We *have* to have that ship. Damage it if you must, but get it for us. Or –" He stopped abruptly, his face flushed.

Paul was watching him from behind an equivocal half-smile.

"Or what, Chaucer?" His voice was sardonic, provocative. "Or you'll take mine? Be your age. You can't take 'Gyr' off me, and you couldn't handle her if you did. Shall I let you into a secret? When I die, 'Gyr's' clocks will run down. She'll live just long enough to wreak vengeance on anyone close enough to have contributed to my demise and then she'll self-destruct. If you kill me, my ship will raze Mithras."

Chaucer shook his head, but belief showed in his eyes.

Paul laughed, without humour. "I keep telling you, you've been out of space for too long. Technology has got sophisticated in the last twenty years."

"Then why can you not capture that tin-can of a ship for us?" demanded Chaucer, his voice plaintive with frustration.

"Because people are the same as they always were, and technology has no answer to brave men with nothing to lose." He paused, frowning. "Unless –" Purpose sparked in his eyes and quickened his fingers on the console. "'Griffin', this 'Gyr'. I have an offer for you. I'll take your ship in exchange for your lives. You have a lifeboat there? – use it. You might be picked up, or you might make some habitable world before your supplies run out, but if not you can still have that clean death you prize so highly, just by opening the door."

Long silences spun webs around both cockpits. Paul was conscious of Chaucer's eyes but did not deign to meet them. Eventually Meredith said, "I'll have to give that some thought," and tuned out. "Quasar Griffin" continued her futile flight into the darkness. "Gyr", having already overhauled her prey, now formated upon her, the black bat hung like an incubus over the silver victim.

Chaucer nodded slow approval and stood up, taking advantage of the hiatus to stretch his legs. He was stiff with tension. "Yes," he said, "neatly done. And once they are safely away from the ship we can destroy them at our leisure."

Paul regarded him without expression. "Once you have command of the 'Griffin' you can do with them anything you like; always assuming you can still find them. I shall deliver 'Griffin' to Amalthea back at Mithras. If your people remember anything of their former trade you might learn to fly her in a week or not much more. If it matters to you, you can try hunting them down then – any competent clairvoyant could tell you where to start looking."

A broad spectrum of emotions played across Chaucer's florid features. Anger yielded in turn to exasperation, disappointment, incomprehension, slow understanding and curiosity. A red light like candle-glow shone and then faded in his piercing eyes before he finally spoke. "You are not going maudlin on me, are you, Paul?"

The mercenary glowered. "You hired me to fight a war, not carry out an execution. I didn't promise you the ship: if you want her you'll have to settle for the deal on offer. I can still blow it up, but I can't outmanoeuvre a vessel that's only interested in running away." His eyes were steady on the screen that showed "Griffin's" position beneath him – beneath was, of course, a purely subjective judgement – watching for any sudden sneaky attack or bid for freedom, but out of their corners he could see Chaucer prowling behind him. He did not like that, but ordering the Mithraian to his seat would have no likely effect besides betraying to him Paul's unease.

Chaucer said, "I appreciate the difficulties." His well-modulated voice had gone silken. Paul had to fight to keep from looking round. The soft measured steps behind him raised the hairs up the back of his neck. "I just have my doubts about the way you are tackling them. Surely, Paul – surely by everything, if indeed there is anything, you hold sacred – you are not squeamish about killing people?" He gave a low, musical chuckle. "No answer. Then tell me this, mercenary – you who hold death on a chain: how many people have you actually killed?"

Paul responded with a promptness that suggested neither pride nor guilt so much as the constant dwelling of the matter in the forefront of his mind. His eyes did not flicker from the screen. "Anything up to twenty thousand." His voice was as bleak as the wind of winters Chaucer had all but forgotten.

Shock jolted the Chancellor to his heels. His ponderous body froze in mid-space; his mind froze too. His round stunned eyes, denied any other purchase on the man whose back remained resolutely turned, found an imperfect reflection in the perspex screen and his face was set in hard planes like stone.

His mind belatedly catching up with his ears Chaucer thought, with a surge of hope that he did not understand, that perhaps the figure was arbitrary, chosen for effect. But even wanting to very much, he could not sustain the theory in the face of the cold basilisk stare in the perspex and the hanging silence, which was such that he could hear his own heart-beat and the breathing of both of them, under and undisturbed by the busy chatter of computer tape and the blip of radar. He was left with the appalling conviction that Paul had answered his taunt with nothing more than the truth. Finally finding a voice, though it was not one his closest friends would have recognised, he whispered, "How?"

"It's not difficult," said Paul. "All you need is a city of twenty thousand people and the means of blowing it up."

"And a reason?"

"Oh, reasons are easily come by. Money's not a bad one. Self-preservation is even better."

"You would kill twenty thousand people for *money?*"

Paul's lip curled in the reflection. "You're hiring me to kill people: that could be considered even less noble. But no, to be strictly accurate, that was not the way of it. I sacrificed them in the cause of saving myself; I got into the position of having to make that choice for money, or more precisely still for this ship. Which was no mean recompense for the deed, though whether it was worth it would depend on how much imagination an individual had, and therefore how many nightmares."

"And do you have nightmares?"

"Never," Paul said firmly. He looked up at last. Half the colour had gone from Chaucer's rosy face so that he looked tired and ill. Paul, who through worrying it had finally rounded the corners of the monstrous thing, felt again vicariously the pangs of their virgin sharpness. He sneered. "You want to tell me how many people you've killed, Chaucer?"

Chaucer regarded him sideways. There was a strange kind of respect in his eyes, and a strange kind of compassion. "I defer to your superiority on the question of scores."

Paul's teeth showed in a savage gleam no-one could have mistaken for a smile, even one of his. "Don't be so anxious to concede. Any five-figure bid has got to be competitive. After all, I don't actually know how many people died in Chad, only that there were up to twenty thousand there before the explosion and no city left afterwards. I didn't actually go back and count the bodies."

"I can imagine," Chaucer said hollowly.

"I warned you about that," said Paul. "Imagination."

In the long naked hull of the "Quasar Griffin", helpless as a sleeper beneath the hovering menace of a vampire, Meredith was sprinting beneath the mess and the flight-deck. He had been conducting a straw poll of his men's views. Breathless and dishevelled, sweating not only from exertion, he dropped into his seat and jabbed his console. "'Gyr', are you still there?"

"You thought I might go away?"

"Not thought; not thought, exactly." Meredith sighed. "All right, how do we set about it?"

"Couldn't be simpler," said Paul. "You take whatever survival rations you can pack on board your lifeboat and abandon ship. When you're clear I shall inspect the 'Griffin', and if I find you've left any souvenirs I shall come after you, pick your hull apart rivet by rivet, and make a small new asteroid belt of your treacherous carcases as a warning to spacemen yet unlaunched. Is that quite clear?"

"Perfectly," snapped Meredith. "How long have we got to embark the lifeboat?"

"As long as it takes. How many are you?"

"Nineteen."

For a slender moment Chaucer did not appreciate that his fiction had foundered. He realised first that he had trouble, then what it was, when Paul said tersely, "Say again," and his eyes stabbed up from the screen and impaled the Mithraian where he stood.

"Nineteen, nineteen," Meredith repeated irritably. "How many men do you think it takes to fly a floating warehouse?"

There was something unholy in the stillness of Paul's body, the even tenor of his voice and the overt, slightly sardonic appraisal of his flecked gaze running over Chaucer like tongues of flame. He held the Chancellor with his eyes and addressed Meredith. "The lord Chaucer, Chancellor and Leader of the Council of Mithras, who is beside me, had the idea there were rather more of you."

"We were twenty," growled Meredith, "until the lord Chaucer, Chancellor and Leader of the Council of Mithras, murdered my midshipman trying to do last run what you have succeeded in doing this run."

"Stand by, 'Quasar Griffin'." Paul regarded the Chancellor levelly. "Is there something you ought to be telling me?"

"Yes." Chaucer's beard jutted like the prow of a sailing ship. "Get on with the job you are being paid to do."

"I was hired to kill pirates. But if I kill the entire population of the Hive," Paul said thoughtfully, "who will pay me?"

"You are our agent. Do as we require."

"I am my agent. You lied to me."

Chaucer laughed out loud. "Great heaven, moral indignation from a hired killer! Well tell me, mercenary, how you propose to get your woman back without returning to Mithras – because if you go back after letting our prize escape, they will tear you limb from limb. Or do you intend to run out on her, too?"

"I'll swop you for her, Chaucer."

The Chancellor shook his bear's head. "You might be happy with such an arrangement, Paul. I might be happy with it. But do you suppose for a moment that Amalthea would relinquish her hold on you? Not to save me from roasting over a slow fire. I know exactly my worth to her, and I know it is not enough to outweigh her anger if you deny her now. If she does not get that ship she will want to hurt someone very much – preferably you, but failing that your whore will serve nicely."

He was talking his way back to a belief in ultimate victory. The collapse of his deception had been a nasty moment, when the mercenary might have done anything – from killing him to shooting up the Hive with his terrible guns. But the time for fury was past. Cool logic had supervened, and Chaucer was confident that there was no logical answer to his argument. Chaucer had built his career on an agile intellect backed by utter ruthlessness. But that had been among men less intelligent and on the whole more scrupulous than himself, and Paul did not suffer from those handicaps.

Frowning, too preoccupied to rise to the threat, Paul said, "Amalthea wanted me to destroy the 'Griffin'. It was my suggestion that I should try to capture it. Ah –"

"Yes. We thought it would sound more plausible coming from you. We were fairly sure you would think of it sooner or later, but if not we were prepared to prompt you."

"It was clever," admitted Paul. "Imagine anything so improbable so nearly succeeding. And yet discovery depended in a fairly long and lucid communication between me and 'Griffin' which neither of us had any reason to pursue; each of us thinking we understood the nature of the engagement, when in fact I believed they were the aggressors and they believed I knew they weren't. That's why you came: to protect that misunderstanding for as long as maybe. And if 'Griffin' had opened fire I'd have killed everyone on board and never known the difference."

"The difference does not signify," said Chaucer. "It is, of course, as you surmise: the ship is no more than she appears, a semi-armed merchantman opening a new route between Feraux and the Ark Worlds. They used a turn round the back of Mithras to pick up speed for the home straight. They also picked up our first distress call. We almost had them then: Amalthea was inconsolable when they escaped. That ship is big enough to take all our people and all our garnered wealth back to those regions where it will serve us as it should. Also, Amalthea has an empire to reclaim. You understand – we must have the ship.

"We knew they would be back – from what they knew of us there was no reason for them to abandon the route – but they did not know to expect you. Yes, we brought you here under false pretences, but that alters nothing. Not for them: they know why they are dying. Not for us: for though preying upon passing merchantmen may be widely considered reprehensible we are little moved by such conventions. And least of all you, because while bounty-hunting is a business of doubtful ethics most people would agree with you, that self-preservation takes priority. That is now your only choice: take the ship or take the consequences. You have killed up to twenty thousand people. What are another nineteen?"

Their strange eyes met and held, Chaucer's diamond-points drilling against the impervious obsidian under the mercenary's hawk-hooded lids as if mining for the gold flecks there. The silence between them stretched and hummed like a lute string. Slowly, Paul began to smile. Chaucer smiled too, broadly, breathing a small and, he hoped, inconspicuous sigh of relief. Paul said, "I am a man of perverse ideologies."

To "Quasar Griffin" he said, "On your way."

The blanket of space enveloping the two craft seemed to pulse with shock. "No!" spat Chaucer, flames racing up his face.

"What?" demanded Meredith.

"Go. Depart in peace. Shift your burners out of here. Only do me a favour and find another way to the Ark Worlds." Under the delicate play of his fingers across the controls the black bat lifted clear of the victim it had been covering and swung off into the oblivion between the stars.

The concussion of her engines washed over the "Quasar Griffin" so that her crew clapped hands to affronted ears. When the shock-wave passed Van Tauber said, "Where the hell is she?" The screen was empty. He keyed up successive angles but the perspex remained stubbornly unfigured.

"He's gone," Welland explained succinctly.

"The cunning bastard's getting a new drop on us."

"There was something wrong with the one he had?"

Meredith said in a low voice, "You may be speaking of the only reasonable man on Mithras, young Pieter. Be respectful."

Van Tauber shook his blond head. "It's a trick. Why else should he pull off? He had us cold – dead. Run a search for him, Ray, he must be there somewhere."

"You're wrong, Pieter," said Welland. "He's gone."

"I'll believe you back on Feraux," grunted the gunner.

"Back on Feraux I shan't believe any of this happened," Meredith vouchsafed reverently. "But right now I believe in miracles."

On the flight-deck of the battle-cruiser, surging into the spangled night at a speed which distorted the familiar images of the stars beyond all recognition, Paul was staring into the muzzle of a weapon he should have known Chaucer would have, and though Chaucer was visibly quaking with rage his gun-hand was steady. His voice was very low, full-timbred with emotion. He said, "Give me one good reason why I should not kill you."

Paul shrugged. "I already have. 'Gyr' would destroy the Hive."

"Give me one good reason why I should believe you."

Paul smiled. He always smiled at the wrong things. "I'm not worried."

Watching him over the gun in his extended hand, frowning, Chaucer strove for some kind of understanding, of the action or the man. Understanding eluded him, but he reached a decision. "Then you should be," he said quietly, and the gun coughed.

Chapter Four

With a shriek, Shah awoke to a place she could not have identified even with all her wits about her. She had not. She had a lead slug lodged in her shoulder, she was in pain, she was fevered, and enough sweat had poured from her to soak not only her own clothes but those of Michal who held her. She sweated still.

"Try not to move," murmured Michal.

"Where – what –" Shah was aware that she was not making much sense and made an effort to concentrate. Her head ached abominably. Her vision dimmed in pulses. All her right side was a stiff and swollen misery laced with sharp pain that stabbed when she breathed, and when Michal eased his cramped body under her. She ran her tongue over her hot lips. "What happened?"

"You were shot. That —" Michal's vocabulary proved insufficient to the task so he started again. "Balrig shot you. He must have been waiting for us. Please do not talk, Shah, help is coming."

"Help?"

When Michal grabbed her by the hand and dragged her, still falling, back into the cover of the hated green, he made his choice between the two worlds available to him; perhaps not consciously but irrevocably. He could have left her and walked back to the Hive, trusting to the immunity that Amalthea's patronage still afforded him. He could have waited until Balrig left and then sought help to take Shah to the Hive infirmary. He did neither. He took her to the forest.

The briars of the hedge which had all but strangled him coming and sullenly scratched him going now snapped out of his way like cut elastic, offering no obstacle. On later consideration he found the idea of helpful plants hardly less disturbing than inimical ones, but at the time he gave it no thought, having his mind and his hands already full to capacity. Michal dimly remembered video shows in which brawny heroes were forever sweeping helpless maidens into their arms without turning a hair. Perhaps through lack of practice, Michal found it harder.

He expected to have trouble finding the Drones and more making them understand what had happened. In fact they found him.

Once through the hedge he pushed on, as fast as he could go with Shah now unconscious in his grasp, into the grey wood. He did not expect Balrig, or any Mithraian, to follow, but then he had not expected to find Balrig so close to the hedge or to see him shoot the mercenary's woman. When he could go no further for the pounding of his heart and the rasping of his breath and the muscle-cramps and the blinding sweat, he dragged to a halt in the gathering gloom and, with a familiarity he would have dismissed as outrageous only hours before, leaned back against a tree-trunk, taking Shah's inert weight on his spread knees.

His head bent over her, despair and salt sweat bringing tears to his eyes. It was over, ruined: his dream of escape, his hope of a future, all his optimism founded on the quick grin of a young woman he hardly knew. Now he belonged nowhere – not in the Hive, not in the forest, and the woman he would have made his country was dying in his arms. Her right breast, shoulder and hanging arm were drenched with the blood still leaking from her wound, from which the short fletched prod protruded like a wicked growth. He could have pulled the prod out, though not as easily as he thought he could, but it would have left its leaden gift deep in her body to fester and poison. He did not know what to do. He thought there was nothing he could do to save her, and probably he was right.

He looked up suddenly, blinking his eyes clear, conscious of scrutiny. Like spectres of the deepening twilight, Drones surrounded him: a ring of the sturdy brown creatures hung with grey rags, binding him to the tree. They had gathered in silence, and in solemn silence they watched him. They made no move. He was afraid of them. He tightened his grip on Shah and, weary as he was, would have tried to shoulder through them, but one of the Drones stepped silently forward and put out his big hand that could hardly master a paint-brush and gently stroked Shah's hair. Shah spoke.

Michal almost dropped her with shock. Her voice was not her voice. The sound and the pitch were hers, and the breathiness of effort, but the accent and the emphasis and the words themselves belonged to another. Michal's skin crawled with invisible ants. Shah's shut eyes did not flicker. All her face was white and still except for her lips.

"Give her to us. We will tend her."

It was the eeriest thing Michal could remember, listening to a woman talking about herself as if she was not there. He did not hand her over but was in no state to prevent them taking her. The Drone who had touched her now put his strong brown arms under Shah's shoulders and thighs and walked away with her, her long limbs dangling, the burden making no visible difference to his stride.

Michal, his reason for staying on his feet removed, sank slowly down the tree onto one knee. The Drones were filing away. The last of them looked back and stopped, and came back for him. Michal accepted the brown hand gratefully, let the Drone help him up and went with the small grey men. Dark fell entirely.

The Drones took them to a place deep in the wood, where the trees were great-boled and ancient and no pollution of the Mithraians' colony had penetrated. Struggling along in the tail of the procession, exhausted and enervated from effort and reaction, mind and body numb, Michal would have been grieved to know that they considered him a pollution, though strictly speaking they were right. Several times in the weary march Michal strove to impress on the silent company the urgency of the situation, that while the woman lived the time separating her from skilled attention was of critical importance. The Drones simply waved soothing hands at him and neither hastened nor broke their pace; and since the Mithraian's ten per cent longer legs were hard pressed to match the ground-covering capacity of the short bent brown ones of the forest dwellers in their own environment, it was perhaps as well that his pleas for haste were disregarded.

They came at last to the Mecca of the Drones' pilgrimage. At first Michal, raising his drooping head to see why they had stopped, thought it was a building. But like everything else in the forest, the great structure was living wood, strong with the sap of centuries, venerable in antiquity. Over generations a crown of trees had grown together, their broad trunks shoulder to bulwark shoulder, their high branches plaiting a lofty roof over the chamber thus enclosed. A narrow lancet doorway twice the height of a man gave sole access. No light pierced the green ceiling. One of the Drones struck a tinder. They carried Shah inside. Michal followed.

The Drone laid Shah gently on the humus-rich ground. It did not seem to occur to him that any softer bed could be provided or desired. He stroked broad fingers delicately across her brow, damp and hot with fever. Her lips moved. She whispered, "Rest. Do not fear. We shall bring help."

"Help?" asked Shah in her own voice, hours later.

"The Drones," Michal explained lamely. "They brought us here. They said they would bring help." He glanced around, huntedly. "I do not know where they have got to."

Shah's breathing, deliberately shallow, whispered in her throat. "They spoke to you?"

Michal winced, remembering. "In a way."

"My head hurts," whined Shah. She moved it fretfully from side to side and woke the slumbering dragon crouched on her shoulder. She whimpered. When the clutching talons relaxed a little she said, "Who shot me?"

"Balrig."

"Who?"

"The captain of Hornet Patrol. The man you humiliated."

Shah remembered. "He's a rotten loser," she observed waspishly, closing her eyes.

Michal had almost reached the point of trying to do something for Shah himself, though the only implement he had was his elegant letter-opener of a knife, when the Drones returned. They brought oil-lamps that Michal recognised as having been purloined from the Hive, and one of them opened a lamp and fed small silver instruments into the flame. Shah had roused at their coming, and Michal helped her to sit. The Drone squatted before her.

"We went seeking your companion at the settlement but he has gone. They spoke of a battle in the sky. We brought things. The projectile must be removed before you weaken."

"I understand."

"Will you trust us?"

A ghost of a grin flickered across her face. "With my life." To Michal she said, "They're going to get it out. I expect it'll be messy and I expect I shall make a great fuss. Please hold me."

The Drone carefully picked the bloody fabric of her shirt away from the shaft of the missile. The blood was old and caking. He slit the shirt and drew it off her breast. He laved the skin. The prod, projected by the small powerful crossbow carried by all the Hive's fighting men, had struck in the triangle formed by her collar-bone, breast and armpit and had penetrated until its lead cap found bone, spreading on impact. The slug was thus now larger than its entry-wound. The purpled flesh had swollen closed on the shaft so that there was no more bleeding, and no room for manoeuvre either.

The Drone's blunt fingers explored. Watching with dread and the vicarious guilt felt by the innocent at others' sufferings, Michal saw Shah flinch from his touch. Then something happened between them. He saw the fear go out of her eyes, felt the tension leach from her body and was aware of a creeping calm that began with the Drones, invaded Shah in a happy conquest, then flowed out and up the ribs of the living chamber like a rising tide. Only Michal was excluded.

What was happening was communion. The Drones had no anaesthetics, nor had they need of them. One person's pain does not stretch far when shared with a planet.

The Drone said, "Admit us." For a moment she hesitated, afraid. But the pain and the weakness and the nausea that came of having a foreign body implanted in her own were enough to persuade her that things could not get worse. She slipped inside herself and opened wide the portals of her mind.

They came as softly as rolling smoke, as multitudinous as the grains of sand fleeing before a desert storm, as comfortable and familiar inside her head as her own thoughts. They came from the far regions of the forest, and beyond the forest, and from beyond the salt sea beyond the forest. They came in friendship and compassion, a healing horde. They took her pain and her fear and divided them among themselves. They were legion; and some of them were Drones and some of them were trees, and whatever the shapes of the bodies they inhabited the shape of their souls was uniquely one. But none was the soul of an individual. The personality of each was wholly subsidiary to its role within the gestalt, the conscious entity born of the life-forces of all Mithras. They were cells in an organism, atoms in an element, and though Shah believed she had understood what the Drone told her under the grey trees, not until now was the full import and all its implications clear to her, the beauty of its simple perfection revealed. As the Drone cut into her she smiled.

Michal stayed with her in the wooden O. The bark gave off a soothing vapour. Most of the time Shah slept, wrapped in a blanket the Drones had brought. They also brought food, and once one of them changed her bandages almost without waking her. Her fever abated. Michal tried to thank the Drone, who only stared at him impassively. He ate desultorily and without enjoyment the hedge fruits the Drones brought, and spent longer carefully feeding Shah slow sips of water. Occasionally he too dozed. So passed all that night and the next day.

On the second evening he heard her stirring and, turning up the lamp, found her looking at him with full awareness and a clear animation in her dark lustrous eyes that he had not seen there for some time. She smiled. "Hello."

He smiled too. "Welcome back."

He helped her sit up. She winced with the lingering pain in her shoulder. She looked around the ribbed chamber. "I vaguely remember asking before but I can't remember what the answer was. Where are we?" Michal told her again. "That's right, I remember now. The Drones said something about it too. It's a special place for them, about the only one they have. The trees focus the power of living things into the earth and the power of the earth into living things. They bring their sick here, and their dead to be returned to the soil."

"Ugh," said Michal, sniffing round him in alarm. "Recently?"

Shah giggled painfully. "Perhaps not too recently. They live a long time. Anyway, the trees and the earth ingest them totally: there's nothing left, not even a nasty smell in a Mithraian's nostrils."

"So long as they do not try to ingest us."

For some reason that bothered her. She was not afraid of the trees, she was aware that they had breathed life into her when her own resources were at a low ebb, but the image Michal's words conjured in her mind was disturbing and she could not yet remember why.

The Drones returned. Shah was learning to recognise them visually as well as by the shapes of their minds. The one who had operated on her, who though none of them had names she thought of as Surgeon, came and squatted before her.

"We have been to the Hive. Your companion has not returned. The Chancellor, the lord Chaucer, is with him. There is much anger in the Hive. They think of treachery. They think of blood. They believe that your vessel will not return."

Shah's newly recovered strength deserted her all in a moment. If she had been standing she would have fallen. As it was she felt strange vacant sensations behind her knees and inside her elbows. She found her voice with difficulty, and it was hoarse and hollow and shot through with fear. "Destroyed?"

"There was no battle. The observers in the Hive saw your craft intercept another. It opened fire, the other did not respond. They flew together for some time. Then they separated, the other craft proceeding on its route, yours arching away into deep space until it eventually disappeared from sight. There was no radio communication. What is radio communication?"

"Something like we're doing now, between mouth speakers." Shah spoke absently, her brain in a whirl. "They use machines to speak over great distances." She stared, frowning, into the yellow heart of the lamp; then she laid her head back against the fragrant bark and stared at the high dark roof. Michal, taking her good hand, felt her begin to tremble.

Concern danced like an angel in his honest, innocent face. "Shah, what is it – what has happened?"

In the pale light her upturned face was without expression, the almond eyes dry and empty, only she clung to Michal's hand as one drowning. His comforting hand was of more immediate solace to her than all the comforting minds in the world. Her voice when it came was thick with gravel and grief. "He's gone. He's left me, the bastard. Paul! You *bastard*! You dog."

"Yes," agreed the Drones silently.

"Pull yourself together," Michal said sharply. "Use your head. Paul would not leave you, you are his –"

"I'm not his anything," cried Shah. "I'm not his wife, or his woman; I'm not even his bit on the side. He described me to Amalthea as his associate, which just about says it all. I'm there when he wants to talk, there to shake him out of his bad dreams, handy when he wants to use me, and easy enough to cast off if it suits him. And why not? Credit where credit's due, he never called it love."

Michal smiled. "I am sure he did not. You would hardly expect him to. Shah, I have seen you two together. If what he feels for you is not love, it is the nearest thing he is capable of."

Squirming on the talons of uncertainty, she rounded nastily on him. "And what do you suppose you know about it?" His eyes fell. His hurt hurt her. Her tone softened. "Oh Michal, I'm sorry, I didn't mean – You don't understand."

There was both hunger and anger in the look he shot her. She was startled by the violence in his eyes. "I understand perfectly. Do not patronise me, Shah. My experience may seem narrow compared with yours, but my life has been neither sheltered nor easy, and there are times when it seems to me I know more of human nature than you and Paul put together. Indeed, for two such clever people you are remarkably dense. You love him and he does not know it, and he loves you and neither of you knows it. All the same, he would leave his money and his ship and his soul behind before he would leave you. If 'Gyr' really has gone, either it is part of his plan to take the freighter or he has somehow lost control."

The unexpected censure had got Shah thinking again. "He's not dead; I'd know if he were dead. And even if he'd walk out on me he wouldn't betray a client – unless she'd already tried to cheat him. Would she do that?"

"Who do you suppose had you shot?"

Shah stared at him. "That was –"

"I know who was pointing the crossbow. But I also know how things work on Mithras. Nobody – not Balrig, not the lord Chaucer, *nobody* – interferes in Amalthea's schemes, not without an invitation. Balrig might have nursed a deep hatred for you after what you did to him, he might have taken every opportunity to show it, he might even in the heat of the moment have struck you. But he would never have dreamt of coming after you with a weapon. He came from her."

Shah nodded thoughtfully. It made sense, so far as it went, but it did not explain why Amalthea wanted her dead. Only because she disliked her? Perhaps it was enough, if she could be sure there would be no repercussions. Despatching her as she left the forest might have seen to that: had she not disappeared back into the trees the Captain of Hornet Patrol would doubtless have summoned up the courage to kick her out of sight among the brambles, and after that she would have been but another foolish unfortunate who strayed into the forest and never returned. Paul could not blame Amalthea for that.

But she had left Michal out of the equation: either she did not know Shah had an escort, or she supposed the Mithraian could not survive the forest even if the alien could. There was some justification for thinking so but, though both Shah and Michal would now be dead had they separated, the partnership was proving surprisingly durable. With a little help from the Drones. Shah smiled at Surgeon and his mind smiled back. His berry-brown face remained impassive, and he faded silently from the chamber, leaving them alone once more.

Something Michal had said, that Shah had hardly registered, came drifting back. "Freighter, Michal? Do you mean the pirate ship?"

Michal bit his lip. He was not surprised, with all that had happened, that somewhere along the line he had forgotten to tell her something important. "Well, actually," he murmured, "no."

Chapter Five

Paul woke with his ears still ringing after hours in an angry, raucous limbo that was neither sleep nor awareness but combined the worst of both worlds. His senses felt battered, like a man spat out after falling through a kaleidoscope. Curiously, although he had lost consciousness before he could identify the weapon, he woke knowing what it was and how it worked, as if his mind had been idly toying with the problem all the time it had been playing hide-and-seek with his body. It was a compressed air gun, and the charge exploding in his face had thrown him halfway across the flight-deck.

Meanwhile "Gyr", without guidance but unconcerned, knowing by his pulse sensor that he lived and unable to discriminate between a sleeping commander and one out for the count, swung on into deep space along the same graceful curve by which she disengaged the "Quasar Griffin". The gun was quite clever, because it would put people out of action without damaging delicate instruments nearby.

Finally, after he had thought about the gun and his ship and his head, Paul remembered Chaucer.

He found him, after an inordinately long search in view of the size of the flight-deck, seated at the console, slewed round and regarding him acrimoniously over the flared muzzle of the little gun. From the angle of the console Paul deduced that he was against the starboard bulwark, from its elevation that he was on the floor, from the way his right arm was eclipsing half the view that his hands were tied up higher than his head, possibly to the mounting strake to which the various instrument panels were bolted, and from the fact that it had taken him five clear minutes to work out a small parcel of truths that should have been self-evident at first glance that his head was not yet operating at optimum efficiency. Also his shoulders ached from being strung up like a pig for ritual slaughter, and there was a deep cramping hurt in his side that suggested the recent application of a boot.

In an attempt to take some of the pressure off his arms he pulled himself awkwardly up the curve of the hull. The effort caused more pain that it relieved, but he ended up more vertical than horizontal, which was good for his self-esteem even if it was bad for his injuries.

Chaucer watched him struggle with no more emotion than he might have witnessed the death-throes of a bug in a killing-bottle. The eyes Paul met were flat and steely-hard, but behind the eyes where only Shah could have seen the Chancellor was wrestling with a kind of admiration. Try as he might he could not but respect the utter stubbornness of the man, his absolute refusal to yield in the face of persuasion, threat, violence, pain and indignity. He not only did not know when to quit, he did not know how. It was not in any conventional sense courage, although a schemer's brain, a card-player's nerve and a soldier's skill combined at times in a convincing simulacrum of bravery; mainly it was his staggering capacity for endurance, not only for survival but for survival on his own terms. He was, thought Chaucer, the sort of man immortality myths were woven around. Death seemed to shadow him like a malvoisin; its aura hung about him but its touch was for others.

When Paul's eyes, still narrowed against the light, reached him, Chaucer said, "I owe you an apology."

"Really?" said Paul; but he was too dazed yet for sarcasm, and he got the inflexion wrong.

"I regret I was reduced to kicking you. I did not appreciate the depth of your concussion. When you were still curled up in a corner after an hour and this idiosyncratic ship was still carrying me in a direction I did not wish to go at a speed I did not wish to go at, ignoring totally my attempts to take command, I began to suspect you of malingering. I was very angry with you. I regret to say I not only kicked an unconscious man, several times, I also really rather enjoyed it."

"I'm glad the trip wasn't a complete disappointment."

Chaucer smiled into his beard, aware that admiration was winning. He shook his head and chuckled. "Paul, Paul – whatever am I going to do about you?"

"Untie me?"

"In all the circumstances that would not be a circumspect move, and I am a cautious man."

"Then you have probably considered the possibility that I can take you out any time I choose, and that short of killing me – which would have the same effect – there is nothing you can do more quickly than I can order my ship to destroy you."

Chaucer inclined his head. "I concede that possibility. That is why I took particular care over your bonds. You will never free yourself, Paul. If you kill me you will spend the next ten days dying of thirst."

"Perhaps." Paul rapped the knuckles of his pinioned hand against the metalwork. "But I have friends in heaven."

They both laughed. They were two professionals, admiring each other's skills, enjoying the contest despite its perils.

Chaucer rose from the console and strolled over to the man on the floor and stopped over his outstretched legs, the big black bulk of him shutting out the light. Paul half expected assault and raised an eyebrow in sardonic enquiry. Chaucer frowned. "I have apologised for that," he said stiffly. "I am trying to find some way out of this impasse. If you have any serious suggestions I would like to hear them."

"It's simple. You untie me, I fly you back to Mithras, I pick up Shah and we leave. The status quo is re-established."

"Amalthea would never agree. She has set her heart on a ship."

"All right, then. I pick up Shah, you pick up some money and I'll fly you somewhere you can buy one. It's not as much fun as stealing, I know, but we all have to make compromises."

"What guarantee would Amalthea have that you would not kill me and keep the money?"

"None. She'd have a fairly anxious few months. Then, unless in the meantime you'd learned enough sense to launder the money, change your name and head for the furthest star you can think of, she'd wake up one morning and find a new satellite orbiting over her head. And God help the galaxies then."

Chaucer regarded him curiously. "Have you no wish for revenge?"

"Revenge doesn't pay bills. You would of course pay for your passage."

"Let me guess. About the same fee as for shooting down a pirate?"

Paul grinned. "That's what I had in mind."

The Mithraian nodded thoughtfully. "It is possible that we could work something out. I propose we return to Mithras and discuss it with Amalthea."

"By radio," said Paul.

Chaucer untied him, but kept the gun. Still labouring under the effects of concussion and constraint, Paul got to his feet like an old arthritic horse. Chaucer offered him a hand. Paul ignored it, sneering round the pain in his eyes, and Chaucer smiled.

Paul called up the navigation computer. At his word dozens of tiny systems which had lain dormant while he slept sprang back to life with a busy chatter. Chaucer marked the contrast of that quiet clamour with the near silence of the racing ship which his best efforts had failed to galvanise. He no longer fostered any real hope of commandeering "Gyr", but convincing Amalthea would be another matter.

"Well, that's where we are," Paul said at length, tapping the screen with a fingernail.

Chaucer looked and saw only random patternless specks. "Where?"

"The devil of a long way from where we started," growled Paul. "How long was I out?"

"Quite a time," admitted Chaucer. "How long will it take us to get back?"

"Quite a time."

Amalthea had watched the shapings of the abortive battle from the pinnacle of the Hive, a tiny finial platform surmounting her private cell. In the early darkness she could pick out the two craft by the reflected light of the set Mithraian sun as they moved deceptively slowly among the still stars. When they disappeared below her horizon she lifted her skirts and trotted purposefully down the spiral to the radio-room to be in at the kill.

She was not sure what to expect. If Paul succeeded in taking the "Quasar Griffin" there would be no dramatic flare of light, no leaping sensors. Perhaps all the watchers would see would be the meek return of the two craft to planetary orbit and the subsequent descent of the shuttle. Amalthea was happy to forgo the thrill of attrition in return for the desired result; especially since she could take her vengeance then.

The Heath Robinson instruments in the radio-room were not the ideal medium for observing extra-terrestrial warfare. They could hear more than they could see, and most of what they could see was diagrammatic. Radio imaging presented a schema of two objects closing, of one weaving sensuously around the other, of the separate outlines merging intermittently as the larger occulted the smaller. A brief flurry of static recorded the firing of shots that went unanswered except by a terse cheer from the avid watching Mithraians.

There was no radio contact with "Gyr". This annoyed Amalthea, who knew that her equipment was adequate and who would have enjoyed eavesdropping on the curt dialogue of challenge and ultimatum almost as much as she would have enjoyed taking part. But she understood that Paul was a professional mercenary who would not relish such close scrutiny of his methods by a client and, with Chaucer up there standing sentinel over her interests, she was prepared to indulge him to that extent. It would cost her little and the small defiance might be his last pleasure.

During the long minutes in which the two craft held station, so close that the Hive's instruments could not separate them, Amalthea supposed she was witnessing the actual take-over of the "Quasar Griffin". The proposal was for both Paul and Chaucer to go aboard and fly her back, with or without her crew's cooperation, while

"Gyr" would return under automatic pilot to her Mithras orbit. Amalthea had wondered about that convenient automatic pilot. It seemed she had done wisely in not putting her doubts to the test.

But when the two craft suddenly flared apart, and the merchantman held steady to her course while the cruiser accelerated beyond the Mithraians' ability to track her and quickly vanished into the stellar night, and did not reappear however much the technicians adjusted their sets, it became apparent that the action had not gone according to plan. At least, not to Amalthea's plan: the possibility that Paul might all along have intended to trick her, as she had intended tricking him, projected her into a dark rage unrelieved by the most cursory glint of irony. The lady of Mithras had no capacity for laughing at herself, and no tolerance for mirth at her expense. But it was so long since anyone had been so lacking in wisdom as to try it that she had forgotten just how exquisitely angry it made her.

The tension mounted by the minute. It became impossible for her to stay in the close confines of the radio-room, humid with breath, wired with high-pent anxiety. Her hand-picked operators were less concerned with what "Gyr" was doing than with what she would do. They expected her to hit the fan and could not concentrate on their work while she loomed there, simmering. She stalked out and up to her cell, and had her tantrum there in private.

When the storm-front of her anger had spilt most of its thunder, in a raging cataract of sound and fury that could be heard through three floors and, like elecricity in the air, felt where it could not be heard, Amalthea began to think of revenge. She immediately calmed down, and her purple eyes grew cunning.

Had there been any likelihood of Paul's return the opportunities for satisfaction would have been many and obvious and her only dilemma where she should begin and how long she could defer the end. But it seemed plain to Amalthea that she had seen the last of the mercenary, at least until she should finally acquire a ship and address some time to tracking him down. For now she was resigned, though by no means demurely, to his having escaped her ambit.

It would have mattered less if the girl had still been in the Hive. From his abandonment of her Amalthea inferred that the relationship between them was more tenuous than she had supposed. But if they no more than casual bed-fellows, scratching each other's animal itches, he must sometime – safe in his distant speeding ship – wonder at the fate of the girl he had left among his enemies, and thinking of him thinking so Amalthea would have gained comfort and no small pleasure from acting out his guilty fancies.

But Shah was already dead. Balrig had shot her and tumbled her body permanently out of sight into the forest. (Or so he had reported. He had no reason to suspect that his lie, rather his anticipation of the truth, would ever be discovered. He had shot the witch woman and she had fallen back into the trees, and it was Balrig's experience that those entering the forest seldom returned.) It was a pity, thought Amalthea, to be denied an apposite vengeance. But sooner or later, however carefully they trod the eggshells, one of her men would provoke her displeasure and she would take out her frustration on him.

She brooded darkly in her cell until the fuming silence and the quaking inactivity began getting on her nerves as much as the pregnant hush in the radio-room. Then she found her fury, while no whit shrunken, had grown chill and biddable, capable of confinement within the cold-storage of her implacable personality, and she took to prowling round the galleries of the Hive like a grim spectre, venom-eyed, contemplating murder down the endless spiral slopes.

So it was that when something finally happened to lighten the thunderhead benighting the Hive and electrifying its atmosphere with poison, the genius of the storm was not to be found. One of half a dozen runners, breathless with middle-age and unaccustomed exercise, checking again where he had already looked, found her in the golden hall, wrapped in her cloak, a shadow behind one of the alabaster slaves.

"Lady, you are wanted in the radio-room!"

Amalthea slowly rounded the figure, substance growing from shadow in an unearthly, inexplicably sinister fashion, and she fixed the messenger with snakes' eyes. "Wanted, Drach?" she asked with lambent menace.

The runner realised with a shock that he could have chosen his words more carefully, but decided that if he could rush out his message before Amalthea passed sentence he could neutralise her acid, even turn it sweet. "My lady – the radio-room – a call. The ship. 'Gyr'. She is back!"

Amazement startled Amalthea's grape eyes wide. She jerked them at the gold and enamel ceiling. "Up there?"

"The lord Chaucer begs to speak with my lady."

She gathered her composure swiftly about her, and the grape-bloom fury yielded to a honeyed brilliance that might have been gayer than the rage, that might have contained more warmth, but was hardly in her face holier. "And there are things I wish to say to him, too." She swept past the messenger and into the corridor at a pace that gave Drach palpitations, but Drach did not care. She had smiled at him.

Paul let Chaucer do the talking until Amalthea began to shout, at which point he cut her off with a ruthless flick of the switch. "Now just you listen to me," he rapped, "because if I don't get exactly what I want out of you I shall flatten that overgrown molehill to a smoking ruin knee-high to a Drone. I'd have done it already if you didn't have two things I want: my money, and the girl. Once I have those two things we'll talk about what you want, but the position right now is that your deception broke our contract and if you don't come up with compensation pretty damn fast I shall start shooting bits off your planet."

A sound like defective plumbing burbled up through the ether. Even this far removed, Chaucer winced.

"Bluffing?" echoed Paul. "I'll show you bluffing." His lip curled in a queer amalgam of ferocity and pleasure as his deft fingers played staccato anthems on the keyboard of the battle computer. Chaucer, wondering if he should intervene, deciding reluctantly that he could more easily do harm than good, thought there was as much intrinsic cruelty in the harsh planes of the mercenary's face, his wary angry eyes and his inapt smile, as would distil from all the Hive if it were boiled down and strained through muslin. Even Amalthea's viciousness seemed petty and domestic beside Paul's epic capacity for mayhem.

All Chaucer felt was a tiny shudder, a faint quiver like anticipation, coming at him through the deck as "Gyr" let slip her monstrous children; but what Mithras felt, after an agony of waiting, registered as a great explosion of light on the screen, and a flat crack like sudden thunder swallowed then in its own tempest roaring like static up the radio waves. While the wild threnody persisted Paul muffled the communicator-grill with his hand. He looked at Chaucer without emotion, only with coals in his eyes.

Chaucer was appalled at what he had unleashed. In his long career with Amalthea he had seen her tyranny met by dismay, fear, subservience, resistance and bloody rebellion, but none had been a match for the Empress's peculiarly potent compound of imagination, brutality and personal power, and he had come to think of these attributes as invincible. Now they had invoked a pedlar in the same wares, and Chaucer could not see any possible outcome to the confrontation that did not climax in a cataclysm which would destroy both the principals and all those caught in the pull of their terrible magnetism. Chaucer was afraid. He recognised the alien state with a shock, more of surprise than shame, and then guilt because one of these world-eating monsters he had helped to create and the other he had conjured out of the stars.

He looked at the dying glare on the screen, dry-eyed, dry-throated, with a bigness in his chest and the still, awed solitary feeling of witnessing the beginning of an end. He said softly, "Was that the Hive?"

"The forest. About ten kilometres from the Hive. Close enough to rattle the windows," Paul added with grim satisfaction.

"There are no windows in the Hive."

"There may well be now."

Amalthea agreed to his conditions, with a bad grace. Paul prescribed the details of the exchange. Not wanting a Fifth Column on his flight-deck if Amalthea tried more trickery, he sent Chaucer down in the shuttle which would then return with Shah and his money. He had spoken briefly to Shah on the radio. She had sounded as relieved to hear his voice as he had been to hear hers. He told her what was happening but reserved a full explanation until they could talk privately.

Perhaps for the same reason Shah made no mention of Michal, although Paul had half expected that she would want to bring him up with her. If that was her intention, he thought, meeting contingencies in his head even as he talked, the boy could come up when Chaucer returned with the price of the Mithras ship. With "Gyr" on station above them and the forest still smoking from the recent demonstration of her firepower, Paul did not expect much trouble from the Mithraians. He thought any residual revolt would be put down by Chaucer's first-hand account of the enemy: not so much Paul himself as his black ship. All the same, he kept his guns trained on the clearing and all his senses on his instruments.

When the shuttle, remote-controlled, was on its way down to the surface he sat quietly among the softly humming machines, alone in his ship, and watched the screen and relished the stillness and wished it would end.

In a matter of hours, he thought, "Gyr" could turn her burners on Mithras for the last time. The prospect of deep space was attractive. It was a pity that he would have to share it with Chaucer for a time, but at the first planet they came to with a space mercantile economy the contract would be complete. Paul would be glad to see the back of it. It had worked out all right in the end, but it had left a sour taste in his mouth that he could neither wholly explain nor wholly swallow.

He had been a mercenary soldier all his adult life. He knew that clients were more dangerous than adversaries. He realised that he had expected better of star-dwellers, and he now recognised that as naïve to the point of foolishness. The recognition surprised him. He had seen himself in many lights, most of them unflattering. He knew he was cold, arrogant, implacable, occasionally vicious, always intolerant and habitually unkind. He had not realised he had weaknesses too.

Next time, he thought, shrugging off the sense of disappointment, he would pay more heed to Shah, take on nothing until she was satisfied. At least that way he should have only one enemy at a time to contend with. He still believed that war fought between professional champions equipped to the limit of their art was a better, cleaner way of settling disputes than involving whole generations and gross planetary products in messy, disorganised amateur skirmishing that could last years and leave nothing for the eventual victors to inherit. Only next time he would be sure of his cause. And he would keep Shah with him. The risks they faced in "Gyr" were easier to evaluate and simpler to deal with than the potential hazards of splitting up. If Shah had been aboard when he had discovered the true identity of the "Quasar Griffin" he would have booted Chaucer out of the side door, loosed a leash of target-seekers at the Hive and marked the lost fee down to experience.

Alone in the quiet familiar cockpit, attuned to its resonances, at home amid its technical complexities and bright inhuman perfections as a despot in his palace or a deity in his temple, Paul felt his sense of proportion, which was not the most robust of his faculties, beginning to reassert itself. After all, apart from briefly losing control of the situation, he had lost nothing. How must Amalthea feel? How would she feel if Shah insisted on bringing Michal with her? Paul grinned at her imagined chagrin but only for a moment, after which it occurred to him to wonder how he would feel. He considered that in some depth but failed to reach a conclusion before "Gyr" shivered to the gentle capture of the returning shuttle.

Even at this late stage, believing the battle won, he did not allow himself the luxury of carelessness. He channelled the communicator through to the shuttle before opening the air-lock. "Shah?"

The voice came back vibrant with a chuckle. "Who else?" It felt like weeks since he had seen her.

"Alone?"

"Except for these." She rattled something glassily, like marbles, by the intercom.

Paul smiled a small, satisfied, almost smug smile at his instrument-panel and opened the hatch and waited for her soft step on the deck.

She came in with a rattle of gems like castanets and tossed the leather pouch over his shoulder onto the console, and wrapped friendly arms around his neck while his fingers worried open the precious sack. He whistled reverently and poured a glittering stream out on his hand.

Claws raked his throat. Shocked to his soul, with awful sick premonitions lurching in his breast, he let the jewels fall and scatter unheeded across the deck. He grabbed the friendly twining arms away from his burning throat and found the slender hands decorated with black talons. In the screen before him laughed the pointed face and the grape-bloom eyes of the woman behind him.

He tried to rise but all his strength had flown, incredibly fast. Amalthea freed herself from his grasp casually, without effort. He tried to speak, but what emerged from the hell-fires blazing around his larynx was only a blood-choked whisper which the computer refused to recognise as his; and Paul's last thought, as consciousness pitched head-first into a cauldron of pain, helplessness, fear and a graphic understanding of how he had been tricked, was that he did not blame it.

Truth

Chapter One

Shah woke instantaneously to panic of a kind she did not understand and on a scale that made its emanation from and containment within a human spirit prodigious and disturbing. And indeed, the panic was not of Shah's mind only. It had swept through the forest like wind, swirling everywhere, buffeting things and people and seeming to draw new strength and turbulence from both. Through her own wide-eyed incomprehension and the urge to flee untempered by any clear notion of what from or where to, Shah felt similar shapeless fear like silent screams wrenched from unseen people all around, as well as a deeper subliminal awareness of something greater, omniscient, more furious than afraid, seething on a level barely perceptible to her with a vast inhuman hatred. Like an echo in her body and mind hung, disjointed, the memory of an anarchic moment when the air clapped and the forest groaned and the earth beneath her moved in a fractional tremor she could have imagined but was dreadfully sure she had not.

She was still lying in the sanctuary of the timber crown, the living room was black as the inside of a box, and her limbs were warm and rigid with nightmare. Michal was sleeping close by, his breathing soft, his mind as clear as an unwrinkled brow, the only sentient creature in her ambit who was immune to the emotional supercharge in the writhing air.

Forcing responses from her arms and legs Shah fumbled on the floor for the lantern and lit it. Its quick pale glow up the fluted bark-encrusted walls revealed nothing amiss. She shook Michal awake. "We have to get out of here." Her voice was shaking too and she could not hold the lantern steady.

Michal woke like the primaeval amphibian crawling out onto the primordial mud: with slow, uncertain paddling motions and very little idea what was expected of him. The beautiful clarity of his sleeping mind was muddied with confusion. He blinked sluggishly at the light. "Shah? What is wrong?"

"I don't know – something –" she spoke half-coherently through chattering teeth – "something awful. *They* know. I can't understand. We have to get out – get out –"

If he was insulated against the earthy feelings of the forest, he was not insensitive to hers. Her distress cut through the fleecy residue of his broken rest and his awareness sharpened and leapt into focus. "Very well." He took the lamp from her, and with arm protective around her guided her through the lancet archway and outside.

Outside the lamp was redundant. The dark forest glimmered with a Vulcan light that came not from the sky but from ground level, reflecting eerily back from the bellies of low clouds. Shah whimpered, "I hurt." There was sound too, a sharp mutter like a sotto voce argument and a soft windy roar; and on the improbable wind the fragrant, pungent smell of smoke.

"Hell's teeth," ejaculated Michal, "the forest is on fire!"

The vigour of rising sap in that green and vital place made for a slow and smoky conflagration. There was no question of the flames leaping from tree to tree faster than a man could run, but they progressed steadily despite the humidity, and within minutes of vacating it Shah and Michal saw the first flickering tongues reach out from adjacent tree-tops to lick and taste and begin the slow consumption of the living chamber to which the Drones had brought them. As the hungry fire gnawed down to the tightly woven branches, spreading a roof of flame whose Lucifer gleam appearing through the lancet heralded the end of the tree-crown, Shah's eyes filled with tears and her heart with a sense of bereavement that she understood no more than the panic.

Michal took her hand. "Come on, let us see if we can help."

The seat of the disaster was more than an hour's march away, but the flash had devastated a great expanse of forest even before the fire caught. The trees lay flat, stripped, in rank upon indecent rank of naked matchwood, pointing their broken roots at the source of their destruction and their bare toppled heads towards the impossible safety of distance. The ground beneath them was scorched; black ash cloaked them with the final decency of a shroud.

The fire had started on the periphery of the blitzed oval, driven outward by the force of the blast in an egg-shaped ring of flame, and close in the trees had burnt hard and passionately with the great heat of the explosion. As that initial irresistible fury died away the greenwood and copious living sap began to play their part, slowing the rushing flames to a saunter and then a sluggish smoky trudge that was hardly an advance at all. The precious place where the Drones accomodated their infrequent dead and rarer visitors marked almost the outer limit of the zone of despoliation within which virtually nothing had survived.

Free to seek escape in a way that the trees were not, the Drones dwelling in the blighted area in practice fared hardly better. Their concept of danger was dulled, their ability to respond blunted by the equanimity with which they met death. They had burned where they sat, under the burning trees, while they wondered if they should be doing something about the situation and, if so, what.

Surgeon led a party of Drones into the charcoal landscape, so alien to anything they had known, so painfully distorted, and Michal and Shah went too. There was little they could do, but then there was little any of them could do except witness and remember.

Shah found an old woman dying under a charred bush where the fire-storm had passed too quickly for total consumption. She found her by the frail wandering pulses of her fading mind. Feeling her thready presence like the tiny racing heart of a hand-held bird, Shah stepped aside from the trail of footprints pressed by her companions in the ash and sought out the heat-shrunk creature in the illusory safety of her bush.

Shah had known, following Surgeon into the scorched land, that such a discovery was likely if not inevitable, and she had dreaded it. Like many young, whole, healthy people she had a shame-faced horror of the ugly things that happen to bodies with age, disease and trauma. Deformity sickened her. But when she came on the little ravaged body of the old Drone she found, to her surprise, that there was nothing horrible about it, nothing sickening. It was a sad thing, because the old creature should not have died that way, but revulsion was impossible in the face of the patient dignity with which she waited for death.

Shah knelt quietly beside her and disclosed her mind. "Can I help you?"

The Drone's mind, undamaged by fire or pain, that burden being shared among all her people, smiled like an opening flower. "I require no help, child. But if you have nowhere to go pressingly, it would be pleasant to pass the last of my life in your company."

Convention urged Shah to lie, to make light of the woman's burns and promise her swift recovery. But she could not lie with her mind and, considering the problem, she understood quite suddenly that no such lie was called for. To minimise the extent of the Drone's injuries was to make little of her, deny something which was her right and put the aside the mute testimony of her abused body; and to promise her life was to discount the quiet happiness and undermine the deep serenity and confidence with which she prepared to greet the death which was the organ of translation to that broader corporate existence. The enduring calm of the fading persona was a revelation to Shah, touching her much more intimately than the comprehensive, scholarly explanation tendered by the Drone under the tree an aeon ago, before she was shot, before this happened.

She said only, "I shall be happy to wait with you."

The old woman tried to drag herself out of the bush and to sit up, but though her mind remained potent her physical shell was all but destroyed and could not serve. Shah laid gentle hands on the ruined thing and carefully eased the old head into her lap. "Thank you," said the woman. Her berry-brown skin was mottled with burns too deep to blister and her grey dress had charred away into her flesh.

"Are you in pain?"

"None, I thank you. I feel very little. I am dying."

"Yes. You are not afraid?"

Again the sweet smile bloomed, moving Shah to pangs of regret. "Child, how should I be afraid? Do I not know where I am going? Do I not know all that I shall become a part of? And afterwards, is there any power of heaven or earth capable of coming betwixt me and eternal communion with my land, my people and everything that I cherish? Do not grieve for me, Sharvarim-besh. I am greatly to be envied."

"And – you are ready for this?"

"I am weary with waiting."

Michal, missing her, back-tracked to where Shah's footprints left the path and found her cradling a dead body. Tears streaked her dusty face, but the eyes she lifted to him were murderous. Her voice was thick with hatred. "You know who did this, don't you?"

Michal shook his head. "We cannot know – not for sure."

"I know. Look at it!" she spat. "There's nothing capable of that much devastation on all Mithras. That was 'Gyr'. It was Paul."

"He could not know what you know," murmured Michal.

"Do you suppose it would have made any difference? When there was money to be made, and all he had to do was turn his guns on a worrisome bit of forest and the poor little sods who lived there? And there weren't many of them, you know, and they weren't very bright."

She put the dead woman aside and rose to her feet in a fast, flowing movement graceful with feline savagery. "He's sold himself – body, soul and guns. Amalthea's found his price and paid it, and he's turned her from a lunatic local pestilence into a contagion with access to the stars. A bit of forest, a few Drones? – with his help she'll devastate worlds before anyone finds a way of stopping her."

They gave the Drone shallow burial under the bush where she had sought sanctuary. Afterwards they did not rejoin Surgeon's party, but at Shah's insistence returned to the margins of the Hive clearing to seek intelligence there.

If Shah had wondered secretly on the long walk back whether she had misread the situation, that hope burst with the finality of a pricked rainbow bubble when she emerged through the hedge into the dazzling unaccustomed light. The shuttle shone in its baptism of oil on the landing-strip. "Gyr" had returned to Mithras; as she had known.

While she was debating whether to approach the shuttle, or the Hive, or what to do, the high main door of the Hive opened and a small party emerged onto the broad curved steps. Shah pressed back into the hedge, Michal behind her, for concealment.

When they reached the shuttle Shah could distinguish the members of the group: Amalthea, a big bearded man – Chaucer, whom she had yet to meet – and four fighting men of Hornet Patrol, long languid Balrig among them. Shah was close enough to see the pouch Amalthea carried and to hear it chink.

Chaucer went first through the air-lock, the others remaining on the ground. Amalthea astonished Shah by using the time to polish her claws. Then Chaucer reappeared. "All is ready, lady." He and the soldiers withdrew a safe distance but did not return to the Hive. The shuttle bore Amalthea up into the dusty sky.

Shah swore. "They're going to thank the bastard with a guard of honour!"

Paul stirred to the awfulness of poison in his veins. His head hammered, his skin poured cold sweat, weakness bathed him like an ocean. Yet he supposed he was not going to die, or not yet, or he would not have woken at all. His throat burnt still, and his chest hurt. For some reason beyond immediate recall that bothered him more than the rest of the awfulness.

He wondered where he was. Not on his ship, nor in the apartment he had shared with Shah, but he had hardly hoped for as much. He moved his head, looking for clues: there were none, only a small grey room, windowless, with a bed against whose unpillowed hardness his cheek collided when he failed to find the strength to stop his head rolling. "Oh, shit," he whispered.

Not wholly sympathetic laughter greeted him. He had thought he was alone, but Amalthea was sitting waiting on his blind side. Now she leaned over him and thoughtfully tipped his face towards her with a slender finger whose black claw pricked his chin. She smiled at him, half like a mother, half like a tiger.

He whispered, "You do a good impersonation."

"Not so good," she said, but she looked pleased. She essayed it again and did not sound remotely like Shah. "The radio is deceptive, of course. You expect some distortion. You heard what you wanted to hear."

"It was the hell of a risk."

"Not really." Amalthea took his hand in hers and he lacked the strength to snatch it away. "I had no choice. Being unable to produce your woman as required I had no alternative but to imitate her, or have the Hive reduced to rubble about my ears."

Paul's aching head struggled with what she was saying. "Shah isn't here? You've lost her?"

"No, Paul, you have lost her. Shah is dead. I had her shot and her body dumped in the forest." The crescent smile of her dark lips never faltered. A note of phony regret laced the equivocal voice with obscenity.

Paul's weak body had gone supremely still inside. His eyes were clearing but nothing came to fill them: no pain, no rage. Finally he said, "I don't believe you."

Amalthea shrugged. "It does not matter."

"Oh yes it does. Because – Ah." The breath left him in a sigh of slow comprehension. His eyes slid to his aching chest. Then he believed her, because she had no reason to lie. He waited for feeling to come.

"Yes," she was saying, "we found your little device. We could not cut it out, of course, because then your ship would have taken you for dead and reacted accordingly. Instead we severed the muscle manipulating it. So it is still reporting your heartbeat to 'Gyr', just none of your instructions. While you live, and while you are here, the Hive is quite safe from your pantechnicon."

It had been the simplest of transmitters, but Paul had considered it foolproof. It told "Gyr" that he was alive and where he was, and by flexing a small muscle attached to the implant he could if necessary call fire out of the sky. But without that direct command

"Gyr" would take no action to endanger her living commander. When his heart stopped, all hell would break loose. But if they watched him carefully he might outlive them all. The prospect was like looking down a very long grey tunnel.

Suddenly and for the first time he was clearly aware, as if some intervening opacity had been removed, how many mistakes he had made: little ones, mostly, but cumulative. He had made errors, fallen for deceptions and allowed himself to be out-manoeuvred with a readiness he was ashamed of, and his negligence had cost him Shah, "Gyr" and as much of his life as was worthy of the name. He had spent ten years working for his ship, repeatedly in situations more perilous than Mithras, and now he had thrown away everything he had won because the euphoria of winning had made him careless. He acknowledged that Amalthea was good, with Chaucer beside her better than good, but still she had not deserved her victory as much as he deserved defeat.

Amalthea was speaking again. "You disappoint me, Paul. Are you not going to threaten me? – Something along the lines of 'While I live you will never be safe from me'."

Paul surveyed her from the curiously patrician angle afforded by his position supine on the bed, which was such that he could look down his nose at the ceiling. With her bloody lips apart with anticipation like the hungry pant of a raptor's beak, and her great grape eyes lively with delight, and her clawed hand fondling his hand in an indecent parody of a lover's touch, she was monstrous and mad but also magnificent: a harpy in full flight. There was a kind of appreciation in his damp face, and a knowingness, and it creased up slowly in a smile. "I thought about it. I decided it would sound absurd."

Amalthea aired a laugh of pure enjoyment. "Ah, Paul, the workings of your mind are a source of constant pleasure to me. Well, almost constant. Will you not ask about the girl?"

"You said she was dead."

"Do you not want to know how she died, or why?"

"Jealousy," said Paul.

The mockery froze in Amalthea's pointed face. "What?"

"You were jealous of her. There was a time once when you were young, and maybe then you were a woman and not an eagle owl's nightmare, but that time will not come again. You had to get rid of her. The contrast was too revealing."

Amalthea's lips still curved, but her eyes blazed. Her talons, scoured now of the drug which had floored him aboard "Gyr", clenched on Paul's hand, drawing blood from the palm. She spoke in her teeth.

"Do not think I do not understand you. You would like me to kill you, so that your ship would destroy my city. I shall not do that, not until my technicians can find a way of suborning her computer. Then she will be my ship, and I shall pick you apart fibre by fibre."

Paul considered the possibility. It seemed not too remote. "Gyr" had been custom-built for him, tailor-made, and on the balance of odds he still backed her silicon-chip integrity against the earnest but necessarily random probings of the Mithraians. Still, they were bright people – Chaucer had managed to liberate the shuttle or none of them would be here. They might gain control of her eventually. Paul was surprised and saddened at how little it seemed to matter. He said distinctly, "What did you do before you were a vampire?"

Amalthea, white with temper, threw his hand back at him, rose like a rearing snake and struck him smartly across the cheek with her naked palm. But though she had slapped a good many faces in her time, in this instance the angle was unusually awkward, and as she lined up a more satisfying second service she seemed to see a sudden image of herself reflected in his eyes and found it oddly humiliating. Colour rose from her throat towards the high cheek-bones, giving a depth and radiance to her porcelain skin which would have first amazed and then enthralled her many admirers. Amalthea, Morningstar of Mithras, looked momentarily forty years younger, a girl flustered by her own passion.

His skin stinging under her hand did more to focus Paul's thoughts, prism-scattered by shock, than any amount of clever mechanical repartee. His world, which had been knocked vital degrees sideways by recent developments, now clicked back into place almost audibly, and reaction set in. True to character, his reaction was perverse, paradoxical, diametrically opposed to anything that might have been expected or understood. Shah had once accused him of hunting round in his psyche for ways of feeling that would mystify other people, and there was something in that. It was at once a vanity and a defence. Now, as the feeling about her death came percolating slowly through, it was not rage that slowly filled him but relief.

He had known Shah for a year and a half. She had loomed larger in his life than any other human being. He had never kissed her. He had never lain with her. Without knowing it she had filled his soul, given depth to his powerful, complex, brittle personality, and given him something to care about beyond himself and the trappings of his warrior profession. Her death freed him from obligation. With only his own life at stake he could act now, within the framework of circumstances, as he wished and chose. He could set himself up against the Hive like a meteor against an atmosphere, and let them both burn up in a brilliance of mutual destruction, and he could do it without a shred of compunction or regret. Amalthea had killed his soul. He was a doomwatch machine again.

Amalthea, watching from the sidelines of her own confused emotions, wishing she had not hit him and wanting to hit him again, saw the understanding creep into his eyes, the appreciation of loss condensing in the shadows under his small introvert frown, and waited breath-abated for the cataclysm of pain and grief and savage fury that would be no less shatteringly elemental because his drugged body prevented him from stamping around breaking things.

It did not happen. The storm she expected did not blow over, it simply became apparent that she had misread the glass. Paul was not breaking up with his bereavement, outwardly or inwardly. His brow had cleared and he was returning her gaze and, satirically, like someone sharing in a rather decadent joke, he was grinning. His eyes left Amalthea and travelled over the bare room. He levered his elbows under him and with effort raised his head to complete the scrutiny. Then he looked at Amalthea again; insolently, she thought, as if she were the joke, but she was used to fear and could not but marvel at insolence from a man in his position. He drawled, "Lady, be gentle with me."

She stared at him intently. For the first time, with Paul helpless in her grasp, she felt endangered by him: not by his ship or his skill or his clever mind, but by the strange magnetism of his forceful, obtuse, unyielding personality. She was threatened by obsession, she knew it, but if she cared she did not care enough.

She lunged at him. Her tiny fists balled in his shirt-front and with unexpected strength she slammed him up against the wall. "Listen," she hissed. "This is insane. Shah does not matter, alive or dead; Mithras does not matter. You and I matter. We are the strong ones, the storm-riders, the void-drinkers. The stars belong to those with the courage to take them. We are the favoured of the universe. But we are going to die like dogs on this hateful, back-of-beyond planet unless we recognise the fact that must be sin-obvious to everyone else: that we are but opposite facets of the same coin, as inescapably bound by nature and destiny as the atoms of one element.

"Look what we have to offer each other! The triumvirate of you, me and 'Gyr' will be a darkness such as the galaxies have never known. We are the harbingers of a new night. There shall be no fury like our fury; our rage shall blind worlds. Our hand will stretch across infinity, and our reach will be an empire beyond the dreams of mortal men. We shall shake the heavens, and pocket the fallen stars for loose change."

Amalthea's mad eyes saw an end of exile, her red lips tasted freedom. Lust ran a tremor like ecstasy through her tense excited body and rang a note of mayhem in her musical voice. Urgent with desire, she pinned Paul against the wall.

"You think you do not need me. You think you could do it alone, but you could not, even if I let you go. I can, though. I have done it before, I can do it again, and I intend to. I want it back: the power, the dominion. I was born to rule millions, not a few hundred tacky middle-aged men with nothing better to do than foster squabbles! Do you know what the real pull of power is, the real opiate? Not the wealth, or the honour; not even the power of death – any fool with a loaded gun can take that. No, the real towering power is not making people die but making them live as you want, talk as you want, think as you want; making them finally want what you want. When you have that you have it all: power amounting to divinity. Paul – I can make gods of us."

Paul gazed into her eager amethyst eyes from a range of inches. He smiled at her, as good-naturedly patronising as if she were a child, and shook his head. "The people you meet when you haven't got your gun."

Amalthea did not understand. She stood back, her wild eyes flicking up and down him. When he offered no elaboration she said tautly, "Explain."

Paul rested his head against the wall and chuckled. "Amalthea, I have done some evil things in my day. I have even enjoyed doing some of them. But I am still not so far gone in depravity that I would willingly disgorge you on an unsuspecting universe. Play with your tacky tin soldiers: you and they deserve one another. I'm not going to take you off Mithras. It's as good a padded cell as the cosmos could have devised. Make yourself at home: if I have any say in the matter, you're going to die here."

That left no room for misconception. Disappointment and animosity welled up in Amalthea's breast. Cruel anger flooded her pointed face, but there was calculation in her eyes. The angle was better now. She let fly a prodigious swinging flat-hander which Paul saw coming but could not evade. Landing with a crack like a whip, the blow rocked him sideways, and by the time he had got his face off the bed again she had gone, slamming the door, her footsteps a staccato tattoo fading quickly down the corridor. The room was in darkness. He sat in the dark, alternately smearing the cool wetness of blood from his cheek and checking his teeth for rattles, and the last thing Amalthea heard before she turned the corner was low laughter gurgling in his scarred throat.

Chapter Two

Over the next few days Mithras positively hummed with thinking, most of it about Paul.

Amalthea and the Council of the Hive wrestled, increasingly acrimoniously, with the problem of taking control of "Gyr", until Chaucer finally got across the message that, if not actually impossible, the task was so fraught with hazard that any prospect of success was vastly overshadowed by the probability of total ruin, the Hive reduced to rubble and no-one left to mourn its passing. Amalthea only reluctantly abandoned her claim to the black ship when the Chancellor pointed out that, although it had taken them fifteen years to get it together, they now had a radio system which had brought them close to deliverance twice in one year while third times were universally considered lucky. After that the Council turned its attention to how Paul might be disposed of in such a way that the retribution of his ship might not fall upon the Hive.

Mithras, in its great black-hearted rage at the assault from space, was also contemplating the man responsible and how it might wreak its vengeance. Not knowing about the doomwatch device, because Shah did not know, it was not inhibited by concern for the consequences of its actions, and it is by no means certain that it would have been deflected if it had known. The compound intellect that was the earth, the vegetation and the people of Mithras was very, very angry.

Shah was excluded from the communion. She hardly cared, hardly noticed. She had enough worrying of her own to get on with.

From her knowledge of the protagonists and from the evidence, circumstantial as it was, available to her Shah had built up a comprehensive, cohesive and utterly erroneous picture of events which cast a new and jaundiced light on the whole venture. She believed that Paul had known the truth about Amalthea's "pirates" from the start or had discovered it early on, keeping her deliberately in the dark either way. His failure to allow her the time necessary to assess his new partner had been not rash but calculating. She had no hypothesis to explain "Gyr's" disappearance after the battle – perhaps the merchantman had succeeded in inflicting unexpected damage, perhaps she had secured her escape by trickery, perhaps they had fought across half a constellation until, succumbing to the monstrous bombardment, the great hollow ship had split assunder and spilt her cargo down the starways. Whatever, "Gyr" had returned without her prize.

She had then proceeded to her second objective: the blasting of the forest, in facilitation of Amalthea's desire to expand her colony, her malice against the inexorable wilderness, or merely her wish to see her new toy in action. For Shah had no doubt that Amalthea had bought Paul, with his ship and his guns and his proud talk about the morality of mercenary engagement, for a double fistful of prettily coloured mineral crystals. It was easy enough, she reflected, to be drawn to that spectacular combination of hardness and brilliance. She wondered what would happen now and worried because she did not know what she could about Paul, what she should do, or even what she wanted to do.

Michal, too, was worried: mostly about Shah, silent and withdrawn, of ghostly mien and haunted eye, distracted, restive and monosyllabic; but also about Paul, Amalthea, the forest, the Hive and himself.

Independently of the Council's deliberations, even to a degree at variance with them, Chaucer thought of Paul not just as a threat to be countered but as a lost opportunity to be rued. He could not rid himself of the notion that better handling of the situation, on the part of himself and others, would have brought infinitely better results. Amalthea was his empress and her word was law, nor was he particularly disturbed that his agreement with Paul had been dishonoured; only this nagging sense of waste which he did not understand kept him from sleep. As near as he could express it, privately, to himself alone, it was like seeing a racing horse break its leg – one moment grace and power and unlimited potential and kings clamouring for a fetlock, the next dog-meat.

Almost the only one on Mithras giving no serious thought to his position was Paul. He was finding it difficult to think logically about anything for more than a couple of minutes at a stretch. His blind cell was dark, silent, blood-warm and short of air. His gaolers were not punctilious about feeding him. He slept too much and lost track of the passage of time.

"Gyr" was not thinking, not in any sentient sense, although the circuits continued to cross-examine one another with inhuman thoroughness deep in her silicon synapses; nor was she counting the orbits she made around the small green world. So infinite was her patience that she was not aware of waiting. She knew two things, which together filled her horizon of consciousness: that she was no longer receiving signals from Paul's voluntary blip-transmitter (possible malfunction, possible accident, possible inimical interference, full battle readiness, constant alert) and that the involuntary life-signal was still coming through (heart beating, life present, no action contemplatable inconsistent with continuation of subject life status, weaponry on hold, further information required).

Her consciousness, which was fundamentally different from the human one, was such that she could deal with virtually unlimited quantities of data, but only in the simplest terms. She was capable of apparently complex, in reality only very fast, feats of deduction but quite incapable of inference. In the absence of further input she was powerless to guess what might have befallen Paul and unable to initiate a programme to find out. While the life-signal continued to reach her she would continue to wait, all triggers metaphorically cocked by electronic digits that grew neither tired nor itchy. If the life-signal ceased she would instantly, impassionately, unrelentingly rain havoc from the skies. After that she would self-destruct, which would be a spectacular sight for anyone still in a position to enjoy it.

It was against that background of fermenting thought that Michal, hating himself, tentatively approached the main Hive door at the top of the curved steps to seek an audience with Amalthea.

He was most unhappy about the errand that brought him there, but judged it marginally the lesser of two evils. He could have refused to co-operate, at least until he should be compelled, but Mithras had made it clear that before that it would use Shah. Knowing the forest's intentions, Michal would not subject her to that ordeal. Necessarily Mithras had instructed him through Shah, but in that cataleptic state, like a ventriloquist's dummy, of which she retained little conscious memory. He would not have her learn the full implications of the Mithras sanction while there remained any chance of keeping her in ignorance. So Michal shouldered the loathsome duty himself, knowing as he did that it was only a matter of time before she stumbled across the truth – in his mind or another's – and only hoping that it would all be over by then.

He dragged his heels across the open space that only days ago had been all his world, deriving brief cheer from the distinct possibility that Amalthea would cut him down before he could open his mouth and thus rescue him from an invidious situation. But she did not. She received his reluctant embassy in frigid silence, but spring set in as he leadenly explained the proposition, and by the time he had finished the thaw was well advanced. She sent for Chaucer, and Michal repeated his message; then Amalthea despatched him to an ante-room, as blithely as if he were still her steward and had never contemplated defection. He found that negligent amnesty more humiliating than anything he could remember.

When they were alone Amalthea turned to her Chancellor with shining eyes and a crescent-shaped beam, clapping her clawed hands with rare spontaneous delight. "And they say God has no sense of humour!"

Amalthea, who did not believe in gods, could afford to be flippant. Chaucer, who entertained niggling doubts, was cagier. "I do not like the idea of the Drones having themselves a culture out there.

That is what he was saying?"

"Something like that. The Drones and the trees. I am not sure he understood what they were telling him." She shrugged. "Well, we always knew there was something out there. It cost us enough people, early on."

"But the Drones?" Chaucer was uncomfortable, though he could not have explained precisely why, even to himself. "We have used them as slaves for fifteen years."

"We must assume they did not mind too much. What does it matter? Whatever this thing is poor Michal has been babbling about, it is offering to do us the most enormous favour and to pay us for the privilege. That is a nugget I am not prepared to bite, Chaucer."

"It could be a trick. If the girl is alive after all–"

Amalthea shook her silver head firmly. "No. I raised that boy. I would know if he was lying. He does not do it well."

"Then it really is vengeance? This – thing – wants Paul dead and is prepared to buy him off us?"

"He burnt its beloved forest. We only mined a few gem-stones, and for that it put us under seige for fifteen years. He blew whole chunks out of it. Oh yes, it wants him dead."

"Enough to offer us an annual gem-gathering expedition into the forest in return. If it wants him that badly, what will it do with him?"

Amalthea shuddered delicately. "I think I prefer not to know," she lied. "But whatever happens to him will not happen here, and whatever his ship does as a result the Hive will not be the target. We could hardly have planned a happier outcome."

"We send him with Michal?"

"Indeed we do. Then I think we retire to the cellars for a day or two; or three."

"You think it will take that long?"

"If I had not known what they do not know, it would have taken a great deal longer."

"I will give them an escort to the perimeter," said Chaucer, uneasy still.

When Paul was hauled from his dark silent cell into bright light, before what his dazzled eyes perceived as a crowd of twinkling people (they were actually about a dozen, and they were not twinkling) whom his starved ears considered unduly rowdy, he was afraid.

He did not think Chaucer reckless enough to let him be killed while "Gyr's" doomwatch device still ticked in his chest, but he did anticipate efforts to make him reveal how it could be bypassed. If he had still had access to the suicide option he could have called destruction on the Hive before it mattered. Now his only choices were to tell them and be killed, or not to tell them and be hurt. He did not want to tell them, because he did not want to give them his ship and he did not want to lose his last hope of revenge; but he was not a romantic and knew it would take more than courage and the right attitude. He knew it would be hell. He waited for somebody to say something.

Amalthea, who with her silver mail and bloody smile went on twinkling after the others had stopped, said brightly, "Congratulations. You have been bought."

Paul squinted at her, aware of being somewhat below par and hoping it did not show too much. "What?"

It showed. Michal, standing with the others, was shocked at the look of him: dull and sluggard, dazed by the light, his hands chained. He had the smell of the dungeon about him. Michal thought that the violence Paul anticipated had already begun, but apart from Chaucer's impatient boot and Amalthea's barbed hand he had suffered no assault. His battered appearance was due mainly to the combination of physical and spiritual weariness, some residual concussion, disorientation caused by sensory deprivation, and dirt.

But what shocked Michal more than Paul's haggard look or the parallel scars across his face and throat, scabbed with recent blood, was the blindingly obvious fact that he was not Amalthea's partner but her prisoner. Michal had thought he could not feel worse about all this, but he began to.

Amalthea was speaking. The arrangement with Mithras had quite restored her good humour. "It seems your young woman is tougher than she looks. Not only is she alive when I had every assurance that she was dead" – Balrig, who was among the guard, tried to shrink his great height to evade her significant gaze – "but she appears to have acquired some influence in the forest. She has put together a deal to purchase your freedom. Be flattered: she is paying highly."

The news did more than strong wine to revive Paul's dulled senses. Michal saw the fierce bright life-spark rekindle in his eyes and watched the vigour seep back into his drained body, stiffening as it went. He stood straighter. Michal's heart wrenched within him, because he would have liked Shah to know how she was prized but could see no way of telling her that would not add to her burden of grief.

With a guilty start, as if his mind was being read, Michal found Paul's eyes on him. The power and the penetration were back; the mercenary was, however briefly, back in business. "Michal, is this true?"

"She is well," stumbled Michal. "She was hurt; she was cured. She is in the forest." He managed to speak not a word of a lie and to give no hint of the truth.

Paul's obsidian scrutiny held him just a moment longer than Michal thought necessary or found comfortable. Then his eyes shifted to Amalthea. "All right. What about my ship?".

The lady laughed out loud. "Do not take me for a fool, Paul. With you in the forest I may sleep uneasily, but I shall at least sleep. With you orbiting over my Hive with your eye to a gunsight I should not have a moment's rest short of the eternal one. No, you take your life and count yourself blessed. If I find you inside my perimeter again I will have your eyes."

Paul held out his shackled hands. Chaucer pushed him away. "At the hedge."

Paul raised an eyebrow. "Don't you trust me?"

Chaucer did not smile. "I trust you implicitly while you have the chains and I have the key."

The suggestion that he still posed a threat seemed to Michal to do almost as much for Paul's rallying spirit as the news about Shah. As the escort detail marched him through the clearing his step was jaunty and his chains did not so much jangle as jingle.

Michal agonised with himself all across the naked land. It was a no-man's-land between the Hive and the forest – between civilisation and barbarism, though he could not have said which was which – and he felt the desolation of belonging to neither. By the time they reached the high hedge he had come to a decision, but it was not something he could communicate in public so he plunged into the twining thicket without a word of parting.

Paul paused before following him. He proffered his shackles again. Chaucer, thoughtfully, took the key from his belt and dropped it on the bare earth. With a grin Paul retrieved it and freed himself. He nodded past the big man's shoulder. "Keep my shuttle oiled, I'll be back for it." Then he too vanished into the forest.

It was noticeable to Michal, and no comfort, how freely the hedge admitted them.

Where the thicket yielded to forest, the broad grey boles spaced like columns supporting an endless vault, Paul looked around him in some wonder. "I'm impressed."

Grim-faced, Michal appeared at his elbow. "You are dead, unless you can get to your ship before they come for you. Shah did not pay Amalthea's price, Paul – Mithras did." He waved a spread hand jerkily around him. "All of this. The forest. The Drones. The whole god-forsaken planet. It thinks. It wants your blood."

"Say that again," Paul said, "slowly."

It was not all that slow, Michal's account, or all that lucid, but by the time he had finished it and Paul's questions were answered he understood both the nature of his hazard and its enormity. He had fought armies – he had never fought a world before.

"We shall have trouble returning through the hedge," said Michal, talking fast now to cover the silence, "but if we succeed we should be able to take the shuttle. There is not much of a guard, and only the overseer will stand against us – the Drones will not. Once you are away I shall go back and join Shah."

"What will they do, when you don't bring me?"

Michal shrugged, embarrassed. "Show their disapproval, I suppose. Shah will probably intervene before they get too enthusuastic."

"And what becomes of the pair of you afterwards, when you've managed to alienate both of this world's cultures?"

"I – we – well, I suppose –" Michal stammered gamely but he could not come up with an answer.

Paul shook his head. "I was wrong about you, and Shah was right. But your advice is worth about as much as a filigree beer-can. No, you listen to me. If I leave, you and Shah are going to die on Mithras. It may be soon and nasty or after fifty tedious years, but one way or another – in the forest, in the Hive or hung out like washing on that bloody hedge – you're going to die here. I've brought Shah a long way and it wasn't for that; and I owe you better than to fling you between two packs of hounds. Can we get Shah away without the forest knowing?"

Michal considered, without much hope. "I cannot see how."

"Then I'd better talk to this Drone of yours. Can you find him?"

"Paul, they will kill you!"

"Can you find them?"

"If they do not find us first," muttered Michal, turning away.

Paul was still a young man by most standards, but he had already lived longer than most young men who take up freelance soldiering as a profession. Contrary to Michal's growing conviction, he had not achieved this distinction by indulging in reckless bravado but by virtue of a logic so sharp it was vicious. A little like a computer and a little like a gin-trap, his brain had a talent for calculating percentages equalled only by its gift for self-preservation, so that his campaign skills approached if they did not actually reach the level of genius. He was a very clever man. But although he now thought until his brain fizzed with excess throughput, every step he took into the silent grey wood brought him nearer to a confrontation he had no idea how to handle.

They walked for some hours. After a somewhat shaky start, when he was irritated in approximately equal proportions by his own infirmity and Michal's anxious backward looks, Paul soon found his stride and enjoyed the fresh air and the exercise, the lingering oppression of imprisonment shaking lighter with every mile.

And then, before Michal expected it and not immediately noticed by either of them, the trees began to play their part. Branches sprang back erratically, so that instead of following Michal exactly Paul steered a parallel course where the going seemed easier. He wondered idly whether the boy was taking the denser path deliberately or from stupidity; naturally enough, the explanation that Michal was taking the easier route but it was being subtly shut against himself ten paces behind did not occur to him. Finally, Paul realised that something was amiss and Michal realised what it was in quick succession, but by then they were separated by fifty strides of thigh-high scrubby growth, armed with daggers and woven impenetrably between the sparse tracks.

"Hang about," called Paul, "are we going different places or what?"

Paul was not close enough to see, but Michal went deathly pale and his jaw dropped. He heard the stealthy sound of lithe verdure, and the answering echo in his brain that said the whispering accompaniment had been with them for some little time, unnoticed under the sounds of their passage. They were not moving now and there was no breeze. "Oh no," Michal said sickly. "It is beginning."

"What? What's the matter?"

"It is the forest. It is closing in." Michal struggled to make sense. "It has separated us and now it is closing in. The tracks are gone. I cannot move."

"I bloody can," Paul said grimly. "Stay where you are, I'll get to you." His own line remained clear but it led nowhere near Michal. Without so much as a knife to his hand he bent and broke off an armoured knot of the tanglewood and clubbed into the intervening maquis. A few twigs broke off, a few lay down. As a means of brush clearance it was plainly ineffective. "Look, I'll go back and pick up your trail where this jungle began. Ah," he added in a different voice.

"What now?"

"The path I've just come up suddenly isn't there any more. Funny stuff, this scrub – got a mind of its own."

"That is what I said."

"Yeah." Paul scratched his nose. He looked at the track still open before him. "Do you think it's trying to tell me something?"

"Paul – I think it is trying to kill you."

Paul grinned at him, without much mirth. "Yes, well, others have tried. Not that I've had much trouble with vegetables before. Look, do you think you'll be all right if I leave you for a bit?"

Michal turned on his heel around his small lagoon of freedom. The thorned stems reefed him in but seemed to offer no immediate threat. "I expect *I* shall be." His choice of emphasis was neither arbitrary nor very tactful.

Paul grinned. "Then I think I'll go see what it has in mind. The sooner I talk to somebody sensible the better. I can't argue with a whin!"

Michal watched him go, a short dark figure, oddly resilient, wading away into the grey wooded world, and expected not to see him again. He wondered what Shah would say when she knew, knowing then her own part. He recalled her blank face and her bleak voice that was the voice of Mithras, heard his own protests and the cold reply, and when his eyes cleared again Paul was gone.

The thorn-brake flowed like a tide under the trees, its ragged surface petrified in disordered crests like foam-caps frozen in the instant of their fission. Like a tide it bore its voyager towards its appointed place, and though Paul did not know that place the sense of inevitability was strong. Like Michal he felt menace in the air, so he trod softly and watched keenly and tried to think of something which he had and Mithras might want besides his life.

The scrub tide broke against the lip of a little valley, steep-sided and gravel clad. The whispering thorns like beaters pressed him to the edge of the defile and, left without options, he swallowed his pride and did what was expected of him. The loose shale scuttered away under his feet as he tacked carefully down the rattling hill.

The cut was a dried-up watercourse, the bed of a small swift stream that no longer flowed, or not in this season. Little streams like that accounted for most of Mithras' running water and, apart from the broad equatorial belt of the single ocean, there was virtually no standing water at all. The trees took up the rain almost before it hit the ground.

The stream, running swiftly enough to cut a V-shaped trench into the shingly ground, had ploughed a straight narrow furrow from here to where the flanking trees gave way of a sudden to a close knot of greenery growing over the valley in an arch. Plunging beneath that arch the cut was dark, but beyond Paul could see light: beckoning bright sunlight, unfiltered by the forest canopy. He thought, I'm supposed to go through there. Then he thought, Sod that for a game of soldiers.

He took a sprint at the far embankment and was halfway up before he lost momentum and slithered back. He gained the lip at the second attempt, scrambling the last few feet with his hands dug deep into the shifting scree. With the whole slope sliding away from him he rolled onto firm ground, regained his feet and was hard against the green wall before the noise from the valley had died away. For a minute, until he mastered it, his breathing was the loudest sound in the forest.

He moved away along the margin of the thicket. It was a smaller version of the great hedge surrounding the Hive, formed in the same way. Within its compass there were no trees to block out the light and the forest responded with a growth of swift sappy green, soaking up the sun and sealing off the wound like a scab. The hedge curved away from him as he walked, while over his head it grew back to meet the encroaching trees with a profile like the surface of a doughnut. Paul supposed the wound would eventually heal over and be reintegrated with the forest. In the meantime he was interested to see what lay within the living lobster-pot that was important enough to bring him so far.

The stream had emerged from as well entered the arena in the days when it ran, though its volume was reduced somewhere within and its bed here a mere gravelly hollow over which the thicket threw a bridge. Paul took a deep breath and ducked under the green eaves. He was well aware that, if the arena was some kind of killing-ground, entering it from an unexpected angle would give him only the most transient of advantages, but he could find no other features to exploit. He could have evaded confrontation for a while longer in the forest but saw no benefit in gaining only time. His mind carefully void of expectation, he entered the green arena.

It was a cactus garden, bright with flower. Flame and scarlet crowns decked the great fleshy plants, horny and thorny and pale as phosphorous, towering twice the height of a tall man against the hard blue sky. The fire-coloured flowers and the electrolytic sky were an assault to the shadow-trained eye. The naked, barbed plants silently looming breathed an air of impersonal malice: aloof, alien, extravagantly beautiful, inexplicably but unmistakably violent.

As his eyes adjusted to the glare and the half-forgotten colours, Paul moved diagonally into the garden, cat-careful, alert for any sound or movement. There was none. No-one advanced to meet him. The tension increased until like a stretched string it snapped in anticlimax and he was reduced to calling for attention. "Shah? Surgeon? Anyone?"

There was no reply. Paul loosed the last of his pent breath in expletives and turned his attention on the improbable plants, wandering among them, trying to make sense of their presence as an enclave in the heart of temperate forest. He saw them as a kind of granulating flesh filling in a gaping wound, inflicted at a time and in a way that no-one now on Mithras, with the possible exception of the Drones, could know. They were decades old – perhaps a few, perhaps many.

His foot snagged in the tangled undergrowth of roots and suckers and would not come free. In mild irritation he tugged at it. Then a sudden access of alarm turned him cold and, without stopping to work out why, he bent swiftly and threw the latches on his boot and dragged his foot free. As he did so the woody snare tightened spastically, crushing the strong leather with a force that would have broken his ankle.

Even as he strove to recover his balance he felt, with surging fear and the peculiar horror of familiar things turned vicious, the very ground beneath him come alive with snapping tendrils lithe as snakes that lashed at his legs and caught his wrists as he fought them. He kept his feet under the kraken assault for perhaps half a minute then, hung about with vines like a forgotten statue, was dragged crashing down. The agile roots swarmed eel-like over him, binding his limbs immovably to the writhing ground, but he did not yell until slow dark shadows eclipsing the bright sun distracted his frantic attention from his pinioned arms and, blinking the sweat of panic from his eyes, he saw the great looming shape of the cactus bending over him.

Chapter Three

Shah dreamed Paul's dream. Alone under a tree, bundled in a blanket, her body twitched and muttered fitfully while her soul bathed in clear sun in another country. In her eyes his dream, too, was clear, shrived of the mystery that had imbued that night in the Hive, but no less horrible. The looming shapes that savaged and fed on him were trees – the thongs that held him their mobile roots, the knives that stabbed him avid cactus spines – and in the dream she was one of them. Most horrible of all was the pleasure and the sense of aptness she imbibed with his blood.

She woke panting, sweat in her hair, her eyes groping for Michal, but Michal had not returned and Shah could not remember where he had gone or why she felt so desperately uneasy about his absence. But nor could she calm herself, and so, though it was very early, she rose and wrapped the blanket around her against the dawn chill and wandered off in search of some antidote to the nightmare. She saw Drones curled up under one or two of the nearer trees, but none stirred at her soft passing tread.

Although she searched with both her eyes and her mind, projecting her perception like a pack of running dogs to catch his scent, she could neither locate him nor allay the feelings of dread that rose through her like nausea when she tried to recall where he had gone. Once she seemed to pick up a faint, frail emanation of some distant mind that was not of the Mithras compound but it was gone before she could focus on it. At length, not knowing where else she might enquire, she approached one of the big old trees and, resting her brow against its elephant-hide bole, opened the petals of her mind to its radiation as a supplicant spreads arms to the sun.

What she learned there rocked her like shell-shock.

She found Michal a sleeping knot in the middle of the thorn sea which, its purpose accomplished, had long since relaxed its tense integrity. It had been a prison he could not without shredding his flesh escape when, too tired to stand any longer, numb with despair, he had cramped his body into the tiny circle of ground around his feet and lapsed into wretched slumber. He still believed himself a prisoner when Shah roused him with her toe in his ribs. Fumbling for awareness with his numbed mind and his sleep-blind eyes and his stiff awkward body he groaned, "Paul –"

"No," said Shah. Her voice was cold. Her almond eyes glittered darkly, despising him.

Michal felt the blood rise through his face, not only because Shah thought he had betrayed Paul but also because he could not explain why. "We – got separated. He went that way. I could not move." He showed his lacerated palms, the blood crusted to scabs.

Shah was unimpressed. "Well, you can move now." She strode off in the direction he indicated without a backward glance, and Michal slunk after her like a kicked dog.

She posted him outside the cactus garden. She could feel drifting, tenuous shreds of Paul's mind within. "If you see or hear anything at all, shout. Then you can hide."

"Shah, please," he begged, squirming under her scorn.

"Shout." She walked under the green arch into the dream.

The bizarre garden with its livid vicious colours was wholly familiar to her. She knew what to look for and where to look, and she found Paul as she had known she would.

The vegetation bound him. The horny succulents had savaged him. His strength had sapped with his blood into the ground. That was the vengeance the Drone had spoken of, and that was the richness, and the tithe was almost paid. Paul was facing death, hanging onto his life with grim, unreasonable persistence and no longer any clear idea what he wanted it for. His eyes were open, half-hooded, the pupils shock-shrunken so that the golden aureoles flared in the sunk dark hollows, a startling colour in his bloodless face.

Shah, searching his eyes with a strange heady mixture of compassion and contempt, sweet and bitter as incense, found no recognition, no awareness other than of hurt. Even the raging power of his mind was drained, diminished to a murmur, the great angry essence of him withdrawn into an inner sanctuary where she could not follow and from whence quite possibly he would not emerge. He looked finished.

But he was not finished; not quite, not yet. Her presence, or perhaps her probing mind, awoke some lingering consciousness in him and something moved in his eyes. Shah felt them struggling to focus on her and, when they did, felt the shock of recognition jar his frail captive frame. Dry-eyed, clear-headed, she said his name and his burnt lips moved in hers.

"Paul, you bastard," she said, "I should leave you here to rot."

She could not catch his reply. She knelt beside him, one hand resting lightly on his chest, bared and bloody from the thorns. He whispered distinctly, "But you won't."

"No?" His helplessness tempted her. She had forgiven him nothing, but at this low ebb any retribution she might exact seemed apt to despatch him entirely, and if it came to a straight choice between saving him and leaving him then he was right: she would not leave him. "No, perhaps not. I don't owe you much, Paul, but perhaps I still owe you better than that."

She hauled at the living thongs with no more effect than that they tightened convulsively into the raw welts already carved where their embrace had met unprotected skin. Her efforts must have hurt him, but he remained impassive until the great cactus with its bloody spines began to lean ponderously over them, when a shudder of pure primitive fear ran the length of his snared body.

Shah growled a mind-threat at the giant plant and it straightened back, its spines rattling a disappointed tattoo. The exchange gave her an idea. She rocked back on her heels. "Let me into your mind."

His eyes flared at her with the same fear the cactus drew from him. "No."

"Wrong answer," she said. She forced her hard perception against the portals of his mind until their weakened defences failed and with a kaleidoscope rush of sensations she was inside his head. He moaned and his eyes closed. She felt like a rapist.

She felt the roots and suckers sawing at her flesh, the cool air against her skin where the shirt had been torn away and the terrible weakness creeping like death through her sapped veins. She sent the power of her mind pulsing through all his annexed body, and when her control was total and unarguable she concentrated her still unplumbed faculties as she had never concentrated before. She felt a pattern develop inside her and *pushed* it outwards, and outside her dual form it became a dome of force, a kind of personal magnetosphere, expanding against the menace of punitive, absorptive Mithras with its message of strength and singularity, absolute determination and the demand LET ME GO!

"It had no choice," she explained later as the three of them rested as far from the cactus garden as an hour's stumbling had taken them, breakfasting on fruit. It was the last of the mysteries and misunderstandings they had spent the time resolving. "Mithras had already accepted me as a kind of foster-child. For that overgrown pot-plant to have used its knives on me would have been tantamount to suicide – or perhaps more like cannibalism, one part of the compound feeding on another. The cactus can neither see nor hear: all it knows comes through the telepathic network linking all the indigenous elements of this world. When it suddenly found my mind bawling at it, so far as it could know its prey – you, Paul – had been spirited away and a part of itself, in the widest sense, substituted. With any luck it's still trying to work out how."

"While it is we are safe?" suggested Michal hopefully.

Shah looked at him in surprise. "Good God, no. No part of this bloody planet is safe for any of us any more."

Michal's tragic gaze went from Shah to Paul and back. He was down to his singlet, having parted with his shirt to Paul whose own was in ribbons and who was still shivering although the morning was now mild, and he had the desolate air of something abandoned. "Then what – where –"

Paul shrugged the borrowed shirt closer about him. It was too big, but the bulk of bandages filled it out in places. His face was ashy with exhaustion but his eyes were his own. "Where do you think?" he grunted, gracelessly.

"I don't suppose you have the key." Paul made no reply, but the look he gave her was scathing. "No, I suppose not. Amalthea?"

"Or Chaucer."

"Michal, who do you think would keep the key to the shuttle?" They were skulking on the outer margin of the perimeter hedge, not far from the small glistening craft, waiting for dusk.

"Amalthea." Her steward sounded sure. "She would trust no-one with the one means of leaving Mithras."

"On her, or hidden?" asked Shah.

"What is it like?"

"It's a key," Paul said heavily. "It's key-like. You know, a little metal thing, flat with teeth down one side?"

"I thought it might have been something fancier," Michal said mildly. "She will keep it with her."

"All right," said Shah. "Then who's staying behind?"

"What?"

"What?"

"Somebody has to stay behind," she explained patiently, "to rescue the other two when they get caught. That's how they do it in all the best videos." Eighteen months before she had not known what a video was.

Paul noted a twinkle in her eye which had been missing for some time. "Well, you'll have to go, for obvious reasons. Michal had better go, because he knows the geography of the place. And if I don't come you'll bring me the key to her treasure chest, the key to her bottom drawer, maybe the key to her heart but nothing we can open the shuttle with. We'll all go, and try to avoid getting caught."

Shah laid her hand on his arm. Her eyes held his. "Paul, if it comes to a fight, or if we have to run, will you be all right?"

He glared at her. "Just you watch me."

Once it was dark they crossed the compound, dodging the sentinel beams of the searchlights, and entered the Hive by the basement door used by the Drones. In theory the night watch was supposed to include the technical area on its rounds, said Michal; in practice the policing of the Drone areas was left to those supervising their labours, and since that was a full-time job the interlopers had no difficulty evading scrutiny as they ghosted through on their way to the higher levels. Shah was aware that the Drones had seen them, and that they were perplexed and watching flat-eyed, but she did not anticipate disclosure. They passed unchallenged into the Hive of the Mithraians.

Shah found Amalthea in her own high cell, alone and quietly brooding. "She's thinking about you," Shah whispered to Paul.

"That's nice."

"She's wondering why you're not dead yet."

Michal navigated a route up the Hive which, though it seemed complex and illogical, afforded swift progress and a high degree of concealment. Several times they heard voices – once a great number of them laughing in a communal hall the other side of a curved wall – and twice they fled for cover from the sound of descending steps on the stair, but they saw no-one and were seen by none, and so they gained the golden hall.

It was no less gaudy, no less crass, but seen in juxtaposition to the silent forest, stretching in infinite menace beyond all their horizons, the Mithraians' need to erect some testament to their own worth finally made a kind of sense. If Shah could not admire the monument, she could pity the deep insecurity which fostered that grotesque expression of defiance. The whole Hive was the spectacular edifice that it was in compensation: a brilliant totem at the hub of a tiny, transient, enemy-encompassed world.

Immune now to glory and grossness alike, Shah pressed forward to the stair, her eyes on the gallery and the door which gave onto Amalthea's private place. The lady of Mithras was still within, still keeping her dark vigil, waiting for the cataclysm which would signal the death she craved and feared more than any save her own. Paul would never know, because Shah would never tell him, but profoundly as Amalthea required his death and much as she would have pleasured in it, her celebration would have been tempered with regret even if she alone would have known of it. She had wanted him with a fierce wanting previously reserved for planets.

Behind them, between the gilt pilasters, the great panelled door agleam with beaten gold opened again and one step fell on the ringing floor. Michal spun like a child caught stealing. Shah, her eyes snapping, divided sharp calculating glances between the doorway and the stair.

Paul turned slowly. His gaze was ambivalent, his voice was low. "Chaucer."

Chapter Four

Shah's nostrils flared with impatience. Her eyes glittered snakishly. "Paul," she hissed, "I'll deal with him."

"No. Get what we came for."

"He's armed. You're not."

Paul looked at her. "Get the key. The Chancellor and I have things to say."

"He has a knife."

"Go!"

With a wordless hiss like an angry snake she turned her back and flounced up the stairs. After a moment's hesitation Michal followed her.

Chaucer drew a long silver knife from under his clothes. "She is right. How does she do that?"

"She reads minds."

"Ah." Chaucer's leonine head nodded slowly, as if it were not the most bizarre thing anyone had ever said to him. "How are you still alive?"

"That was Shah, too. Faced with the choice of her safety or mine, she opted for the latter. I really don't know why."

"Why are you here?"

"To repossess my spacecraft. Amalthea has the key."

"Yes." Chaucer looked after the young man and the girl. "Will they kill her?"

Paul looked at the knife, and, curiously, at Chaucer. "Does that matter to you?"

Chaucer laughed ruefully. "Oddly enough," he said, "it does."

"You'd be better off without her."

"I know."

"You should have taken the deal I offered."

"I know."

Paul felt the same frustration that had ridden him in "Gyr", trying to coax the fleeing freighter to stand and fight. "Chaucer, this planet is approaching a state of integrated consciousness. I don't expect you to understand what that means, but the point is coming at which Mithras will tolerate the Hive no longer. There will be nothing you can do about it, the planet will simply become untenable for you. I can still arrange for you to get your men away before that."

"My men?"

"I'll find you a ship, I'll find you a crew and I'll find a planet willing to take you."

Chaucer smiled. "Same fee?"

"Same fee," affirmed Paul.

"What of Amalthea?"

Paul sucked in a deep breath. "She's mad, and she's evil. She's galactic warfare walking round looking for somewhere to happen. Mithras is the perfect prison. It would be criminal ever to let her leave."

"And do you suppose," suggested Chaucer, aiming blind but with devastating accuracy, "that no-one ever said the same about you?"

Paul froze from the soul out. It had been more than ten years, but the nerves still jumped when the wound was touched. At length he said, "I know they did." A tiny spasm he could not suppress caught up his face and his voice. Chaucer was abruptly reminded how much abuse his unremarkable body had absorbed over the past days. Striking him with the force of a revelation came the knowledge that, almost whatever the circumstances, he was not prepared to add to it further. The play was done, and if he was less than happy with his performance in it there was at least a certain dignity in ringing down the curtain.

"Damn you, listen to me!" Chaucer blinked, surprised somehow to find Paul still talking. His eyes blazed and his lip had a hard twist the Chancellor recognised, with amazement, as self-contempt.

"They said it, and they meant it, and they did to me things you wouldn't understand the half of before they felt safe from me. I didn't think so at the time, of course, but they were right. There are some people who are just too intrinsically dangerous to have around. Probably I was one. For certain, she's another."

For a surreal moment, held in the bitter gold-sparked gaze of an angry young man's strange eyes, Chaucer felt himself in the pull of a black hole, an emotional event horizon sucking him into that elemental chaos that was Paul's tormented restless spirit. It was of course a nonsense. Paul was not a cosmic force, only a rather battered young man with more ability than purpose, more intelligence than understanding, more past than future, and the hollowness of misplaced destiny haunting the back of his eyes.

Precisely what spectres rode him the Mithraian did not know, and he doubted that it mattered. What disturbed Chaucer was not that he was haunted but that he should know his ghosts so well. He was become the sum of them: all the cruel and bitter things, all the betrayed ambitions, the lost illusions, the murdered hope. He had trodden the coals of human bankruptcy and emerged, if not unscathed, still somehow unconsumed. Such intimacy with the stuff of death seemed to Chaucer a kind of incest, an unholy alliance of blasphemy and a strange innocence. He felt suddenly very old and very weary.

He laid his knife, which he was still holding, down on a table and turned away. "Go home, Paul – wherever you conceive that to be. Take your key. Take your friends, and your ship, and your money, and go. Leave us in peace."

"You'll all die here!"

"Then let us rest in peace," snapped Chaucer. "I will not have her killed and I will not abandon her. She is all that you say, perhaps more, but we all swore her fealty and were glad to do it, and I will not see her betrayed now. Do not grieve for us, mercenary. We are none of us much better than Amalthea, and all of us less great."

Shoulders set, he walked away down the long hall, rocklike in his immovable determination, but he did not reach the door. From the gallery, where a black slit marked the door ajar to Amalthea's chamber, came a cry of such anguish as to momentarily strike both men where they stood. The voice was Michal's, and the words were "Lady – no!" and in all the circumstances they could have meant almost anything, but the tone was pure horror.

Paul reacted first. His tired body jerked into action and he was halfway up the stairs before he realised he had snatched Chaucer's knife from the table-top as he moved.

Shah had entered the dark chamber mind first.

Amalthea, seated still upon her black throne, her black cloak cast around her, had heard nothing, but neither was she thinking of the key to the purloined shuttle. There was no reason why she should. Until "Gyr" had taken such action as was programmed to mark her captain's death it would be most unwise to approach her, and if that programme did indeed conclude with self-destruction it could be a long time before the little craft would be of use. It would naturally be kept safe against that day, but there was no urgency to keep the key constantly at the forefront of its custodian's mind. It would have been convenient, but Shah was hardly surprised.

She paused inside the door, letting her eyes adjust to the darkness, watching the inanimate things she could not feel crystallise out of the gloom. Then she said, "Amalthea."

Amalthea's mind lurched, dry-spinning at the unfamiliar sound of a woman's voice. She half-rose from her throne before understanding came, and she composed herself. "You," she said. "Of course. I knew you were alive. I just have not got over the disappointment yet."

Shah smiled in the dark. "Work at it."

Amalthea gave a low appreciative chuckle. "You are good. You remind me of me at your age. I was well on the way to my first empire by then. What do you want?"

"Not an empire. From you, only the key to the shuttle. We're leaving."

Amalthea looked past Shah to Michal. Her gaze still turned his knees to jelly. "Can you fly it?"

"I don't have to," Shah said evenly. "Paul will fly it."

Amalthea laughed out loud, a jackal laugh. "My dear child, you *are* behind the times. Paul is –"

"Raw meat? Pegged out and bleeding to death in a cactus garden? No. He's here, but not for long. We're going up to "Gyr" as soon as you give me the key to the shuttle."

"Over my dead body!" swore Amalthea.

"That would be a bonus," admitted Shah, "but I'll do without if we can make this quick, simple and easy. The key. And Paul's money, if you please. He'd have done the job you hired him for, if it had been there to be done. Your mischief nearly cost him his life."

"How *shall* I live with myself?"

Shah's eyes kindled. "Don't push your luck, lady. You deceived me too. Because of your trickery I damn nearly left him to die. Amalthea, if I had, and then found out what I know now, I would still be here but not for the key." Her attention remained fixed on the Empress but she spoke to Michal. "The key is on a cord round her neck. Get it."

Amalthea rose slowly from the throne. Michal approached her with trepidation. The black cloak fell to the floor and her silver body glittered like a fish. He could not shrug off twenty years' worship. With everything she was and had done, she was still the woman who raised him, who fed and protected him, without whose strength and energy probably none of the Hive people would have survived, and he could not bring himself to hate her or lay a hand on her. "Lady, I – I –" he faltered.

"It's inside her dress, on a cord," prompted Shah, wondering what the problem was.

Michal stood between them, indecisive and mortified. His hands made futile half-gestures towards the task before finally admitting defeat. He hung his head in humiliation. "I cannot."

Shah suddenly realised what was stopping him. "For pity's sake!" she exclaimed furiously, starting forward. "She's made exactly the same way as I am – surely to God you're not frightened of boobs?"

Under the spur of impatience her concentration flickered, and with her hands raised either side of Amalthea's throat she was brought to an abrupt halt by the blunt shock of something small and hard pressed under her breast which in all the circumstances could be only one thing, which a quick downward glance confirmed that it was. Inches separated the two women's eyes: Shah's startled wide, Amalthea's complacent and lazily smiling. Shah had no time to get into her mind and stop her before the gun went off.

It was the compressed air-gun Chaucer had taken aboard "Gyr". It had lain Paul out for hours, but that was used as the designer intended, to deliver a concussive shock to the brain from close range. At point-blank range a discharge to the head was as lethal as an ox-hammer: against her rib-cage the blow was enough to hurl Shah across the dark room, her chest clamped in a vice of clutching pain. She fetched up in the angle of floor and wall, stunned and hurting, with no clear appreciation of where her arms and legs had got to and less of where her perception was. Two places it was not: in her own forebrain, ready for use, and in Amalthea's, inhibiting murder.

Amalthea followed her across the floor, without haste, like a stalking moonbeam. The gun hung loosely at the end of her arm. Shah saw or heard or felt her coming and tried to crawl away, panic scrabbling in her head to claw out the confusion, but the corner of the room trapped her. She struggled to rise, but her side hurt and her head hurt and both strength and equilibrium failed her, so she slipped quite slowly down the corner, her cheek against the black wall.

From the tail of one almond eye, great with fear, she saw silver Amalthea bear down on her like a searchlight and stop within arm's reach. She saw the pale bare arm come up, straight and calm, and the silver gun steady in the small clawed fist. She shook her head, tiny repetitive shakes like a tremor, whimpering.

She felt the flared muzzle of the strange gun lodge against her temple, between the ear and the eye where the flat bone made for a good contact, and the cool kiss stopped the shake and the whine and perhaps all the ongoing mechanisms of life, but she heard Michal cry "Lady – *no!*" with all the anguish of divided loyalties.

Amalthea slid him one slow sideways look, without anxiety or compassion or dislike or any other human concern; almost without recognition, as if his cry were the creak of a board or the whisper of a draught under the door, no sooner identified than forgotten.

Michal had never in his short life been a mover of events, but he had served his lady faithfully and then betrayed her utterly, and the certain knowledge coming in that brief moment of eye contact that she had difficulty remembering his face was devastating in a way that even her fury never was. Something left him: not the fear of her, not the instinct for self-preservation; perhaps that integrated view of his world by which the individual makes sense of the things happening about him, in the absence of which neither his actions not any other's retain enough meaning to keep the fabric of life from crumbling and entropy from pouring in. It was in that state of dearth and meaninglessness that Michal acted now, without consideration for the consequences, because it was that integrity of cause and effect which Amalthea's ultimate, largely unwitting insult had dislocated.

Without foresight and therfore calmly, he swept Amalthea aside with one arm and gathered Shah up in the other and projected her – her long body limp with reaction, unresisting but not helping much either – out onto the gallery, where she stumbled into Paul's arms as he raced up the stair.

Almost without breaking step he put her behind him, thrusting her into Chaucer's grasp. In a situation too hectic and too far gone for chauvinism, the Chancellor took charge of the frightened girl as if he had not spent the last several days conspiring at her death. His big hands supported her and his mellow, musical voice encouraged the breath and the heart and the life back into her. Holding Shah, feeling her heart thunder against his chest, mouthing solicitudes that occupied a fraction of his attention, Chaucer thought of Amalthea and doubted if he could do anything to help her now and wondered if he wanted to.

The impetus of Paul's drive for the Empress was broken by the rock-steady figure of Michal, still in the doorway, tall and strong and filling it with an unfathomable calm. But Paul was not interested in Michal and hardly noticed. His eyes were savage with a warning that was little short of a threat. "Get out of my way!"

Michal looked at him – looked down at him – without expression. His gentle eyes were blank, his innocent face enigmatic. They gave no clue to the whirling madness deep within him, the sudden surging soaring sense of freedom. He shook his head. "No."

If Amalthea could have seen her lost steward's strange luminous, prophetic face she too might have been stayed, but she did not. She saw only his broad back filling her door, an unforgivable intrusion between her and her quarry, and she pressed the flared muzzle of her gun against his spine and squeezed the trigger.

After the muffled sonic belch and the soft thump of the boneless falling there was nothing but silence. No cries, no recriminations; no flurry of too-late action; no wailing, no gnashing of teeth. Only the silence, whose very profundity finally penetrated Shah's shock-shell and brought her, tentative as a shy child, back to the Hive, to Chaucer's impersonally protective arms, and to the light faintly ashy scent, fragrant as woodsmoke, of dying.

She turned out of the Chancellor's embrace and, drying her nose on her sleeve, moved with uncertain steps to the doorway of Amalthea's cell. There she stopped and looked down. Still no-one spoke, no-one stirred. The silence stretched impossibly, drawing out thinner and thinner and wider until it seemed to encompass not only the Hive but all of Mithras in its tenuous elastic web. Paul stood beside her. Only inches separated them, but he made no attempt to touch her or she him. When she had seen enough she stepped carefully over Michal's crumpled body into the room. She breathed gently and felt anger and power come with every breath. She no longer felt her own hurt.

Amalthea had posed too much of a menace all her life not to recognise danger when she saw it, even if she did not understand it, and had come too far on the strength of sheer female power to deny the potency of the inexplicable. Her amethyst eyes burned, her red mouth curved with defiance and adrenalin. She stood her ground, levelled the gun and fired.

The range was too long and Shah absorbed the shock-wave with only a sway, as if she had been slapped across the cheek. She stepped forward. Amalthea fired again, but as the distance between them shrank so the compression cell of the small weapon ran down; the effect was the same. Shah stepped forward. Finally Amalthea stepped back. Locked in a kind of slow, graceful, terrible dance the two women – small silver electric Amalthea, brilliant even in retreat, and dark Shah, gaunt and ragged, implacable-eyed, an advancing Nemesis, justice with an invisible sword and no blindfold – glided in unison towards the centre of the chamber.

Premonition struck Paul like a fist to the gut when he realised, with a sudden totality of comprehension like an apocalypse, what Shah intended. Cold jolted through him. "No, Shah!" He hurdled the obstacle in the doorway and caught her arm. "No."

She spared him no glance. "Take your hand off me." Her voice was death.

"Not that way, girl. Not –"

She threw him off. She angled her head just enough to flash lightning at him from the corner of one coldly raging eye, and the force of her mind hit him like running into a wall. Pain exploded behind his eyes like fireworks. His sight went out. His brain felt as if it was being kneaded against the inside of his skull. Deprived of vision and with the strange fierce pressure in his head, his balance began to waver. For a brief chilling moment he lost all sense of direction and elevation, like weightlessness or the jump-sickness that afflicted tyros aboard star-drive ships, or the deep disorientation and confusion achieved by sensory deprivation. He seemed to float for an incalculable time in an infinite ocean of black, without space or time or any reference points, just his small lost mentality, frightened and bewildered, adrift in four dimensions out of sight of land.

Then, stumbling blindly, he lurched against the wall. Its firm substance and uncompromising verticality were a fixed point in the void of his senses. By clinging to that small reality with all the will he could muster he was able to claw a chink in the enveloping dark, like a chick in search of birth pecking a window in its shell, and thence to roll back the shroud with an effort no less laborious for its metaphysical nature. The Hive came back.

Amalthea had cast her exhausted weapon aside. She was still backing before Shah's advance, but there was no sign of fear about her, or even of resentment. She made her slow reverse easily, with a faintly impish smile, as if she found quietly fighting for survival a great joke. Her voice, when at last she broke the silence, compounded the charisma of wit, irony and exhilaration. "I know how it would pleasure you to see me destroyed. But you cannot do it, child; not you. I am your future."

"Then I don't want it," said Shah. "I would not live so long that I should favour you."

"You have no choice. You are my past."

"In all my life," Shah said grimly, "I never had but three friends. The first was my conscience, the best of me, and he is far from here. The last you have murdered with no more point or purpose than a man needs to swat a fly."

"Michal? Michal betrayed me."

"Michal never by word or deed betrayed you. He vouchsafed me his friendship, maybe even his love, but his worship he reserved to you. He didn't think you deserved it, he just couldn't help himself. Do you suppose he died protecting me from you? No. He put himself between you and your proper and inevitable destruction, and you killed him for his pains. So now history can take its course."

Amalthea hooted. "You see yourself as history?"

Shah managed a bleak smile. "Destiny, then; at least yours."

"Child," said the lady of Mithras, her voice vibrant, "you do not begin to know what destiny is. All this" – she waved a white arm round the dark room – "is charade. Nothing important has happened here, except that you and I have discovered each other. That is what destiny is: fate distorting the lives of hundreds for twenty years to achieve the meeting of two people who would never otherwise have found each other. Everything that has happened to my people since we left our home, or maybe even before – perhaps the very existence of this planet Mithras – was a device to bring us together. That makes us very special, Sharvarim-besh.

It makes it a sacrilege even to consider rejecting what I offer."

"A darkness the galaxies have never known?" suggested Shah. "An empire beyond the dreams of men? Falling stars for loose change? Are you going to make me a god too, Amalthea?"

Anger, but still no fear, flared in Amalthea's gaze. Her eyes stabbed from Shah to Paul and back. "Him? Yes, I would have treated with him, until I had his ship. I have always used men. I have never shared anything with any of them. That is the unique bounty I offer you."

Shah paused, but only to seek a way of expressing herself unmistakably. "Amalthea, even if I wanted what you offer, how could I trust you? You are without honour. All Mithras is a cactus garden, knives behind flowers, but you who were not even born here are its crowning poison. You lie, cheat and deal death not only for profit, which is monstrous, but for pleasure. You have a whim of adamant.

"I posed you no threat when you sent a man to kill me. Despite your deceits, Paul was still trying to fulfil a contract for you when you sold him to the planet for a kind of death no human being should have condoned. Your treachery all but cost him his life; and me my soul, for I believed him your convert and was prepared to abandon him to the consequences of that alliance, and would never have known my error while he lived had you not delegated his death to the forest. And now you have murdered probably the only person ever who cared for you unselfishly. You are too awful to live."

"I am too awesome to die," pronounced Amalthea. "At your hands, anyway."

"Hands?"

Close enough to join hands, they confronted each other. Amalthea could retreat no further – seeking the advantage, perhaps more psychological than actual, of the raised plinth in the centre of her chamber she now found herself trapped with the black throne at her back – but Shah made no overt move towards her. Only her eyes went still and chill and somehow deep, vertiginous and unfathomable as sacrificial wells and equally inviting. Amalthea felt herself falling into them, drawn compulsively, helpless to save herself, tumbling like an inept diver with no sense of direction save down. And as she fell she felt pressure growing in her head like a worm growing in her brain.

Amalthea screamed. The terrible quavering shriek stilled hearts and froze blood wherever in the Hive it was heard: a piercing, alien wail woven of agony, dread, defeat and a peculiarly poignant despair. Her amethyst eyes glazed and slid away.

Paul was behind her, to one side of the throne, his right arm about her narrow waist, Chaucer's long knife in his hand buried to the hilt in her breast. The silver mail had scarcely delayed its entry: it had passed under the ribs from the unprotected triangle of her thorax and lodged in her heart, where a sharp twist let out all her life. Her quit body, smaller than always, slumped in his arms. He held her for a dullard moment. Then, awkwardly, lacking his customary strength, he manoeuvred her to the throne and let her down there. Her head tipped back and her dead eyes, already losing their grapebloom lustre, surveyed the room quizzically and with no little irony.

Shah, all her senses back in her own head, mounted the step. She looked not at Amalthea, but at Paul. Her eyes were primitive with fury. She made no attempt to speak. Her arm swung and her open palm slashed against his cheek where the print of Amalthea's claws still lay.

The force of the blow rocked him. His last reserves of resilience tapped to the bed, he took time to recover. He said wearily, "You would have killed her."

"You're damn *right* I'd have killed her," shouted Shah. "She was *mine*. You had no right –"

"From inside. You were going to kill her from inside. You'd never have got out."

Shah stared at him. Her skin began to crawl. "How do you know?"

Paul shrugged. He looked almost as shrunken and wasted as the dead woman on the throne. He looked as though if he did not sit down soon he would fall down. "I don't, not for sure. It was one of the things we considered when – when I –" He shrugged again. "We considered it too dangerous to try. There weren't many things my makers considered too dangerous; except, of course, trusting me with my own brain."

Shah sought his eyes. Even through her own waning rage and growing grief she felt his dull hurt. Her long fingers touched his cheek with the gentleness of a moth-wing in the dark. She spoke quietly but without sentiment.

"What I said, before. It wasn't true. I always trusted you. I haven't always understood you, so sometimes I've made mistakes, and often enough I have disagreed with you. I have disapproved of much that you have done. You are ruthless and devious, and such as they are your morals stand at right-angles to everything I was brought up believing. But if I had to choose someone in whom to trust my life, my soul and all I have, without hesitation or reservation, Paul, my choice would still and always be you. Take my hand in your hand and I will walk with you beyond the furthest bound that men dare contemplate."

Chaucer, watching with a kind of wonder from the doorway, thought they could be meeting for the first time. Their eyes held each other. Lines that had been so much a feature of Paul's face that he had thought them permanent softened and found new, less rigorous purposes: care supplanting cynicism, comprehension finally usurping mere cleverness. Peace descended about him like snow-flakes. He smiled gravely at the tall dark girl with her brilliant eyes and her remarkable mind and her fearsome honesty and, with a strange grace born of economy and lack of artifice, dropped her a simple untutored bow.

Chaucer was loathe to break in on their moment but he had no choice. "Lady, the steward lives still."

Chapter Five

Shah spun, her face ashimmer with hope, but Chaucer's expression and, even more, Chaucer's tone, which she assimilated more slowly than his words, knocked the shine out of her eyes and prepared her for the less happy reality.

Michal was still alive, but only in the technical sense that his dying was not yet done. A hand's breadth of his spinal column had been devastated. His broken body lay limp and untidy across the doorway, bonelessly insensate, the strong young limbs tangled and spoiled. His face was as grey as dust, his eyes almost closed, only fine white lines showing under the long lashes. He made no sound, even of breathing, and was aware of nothing. It did not require the talents of a telepath to know that Michal's body was damaged beyond repair and all of his life was withdrawing inside himself, gathering closer and smaller and further from the world of men. The process would take minutes rather than hours, and when it was complete there would be nothing left of him.

Shah knelt by him. Her eyes were glossy with sorrow but no tears. There was a kind of inevitability about his end that precluded passionate grief; as if, had they but thought, they should have known that a steward who had served faithfully all his remembered life would not leave his mistress, either on Mithras or in death. Shah, who had won so much, was conscious of having lost this last hand to Amalthea, and that after she was dead.

She looked up. "Oh Paul," she sighed, "look what we've done."

"Not you. Not even me, for once. The doing was Amalthea's."

"Only mostly," said Shah. "We all contributed something. The Hive and the people of the Hive created Amalthea as surely as she created it. You could have stopped her at any time," she charged the Chancellor, "but you enjoyed the power she fed you. As long as the Drones underpinned it, no man was so low down the hierarchy that he did not feel to benefit from it: apart from the baseline, anywhere you stand in a pyramid you always have more people to kick than you have kicking you. If you don't care about justice the system is crudely effective, and so the megalith stood until we arrived on the scene."

Her gaze glided round to Paul. "You disturbed the equilibrium. If you'd come and done their job and gone, or died, the pyramid would have stood unchanged and Michal safe within its structure. But you challenged the status quo. You represented the possibility of alternate worlds: better ones, whatever else you are you were never designed for tyranny, but you introduced the concept of choice into a social system from which it had been purged.

"And I made tragedy certain by seducing the loyalties of the one poor soul in the Hive without the experience to follow his heart and still watch his back. Given all the circumstances, Michal was always going to be the victim of everyone else's ambitions."

Chaucer cleared his throat. His mellow voice came out gruff. "If you two hope to get away without unpleasantness, now would be a good time to do it, before this day's deeds are known." He extended a hand to help Shah rise.

Her eyes dared him to touch her. She aimed her words at Paul like pellets. "I won't leave him while he lives." Her tone was defiant.

Paul looked at the dying man. His face caught up in a small, possibly unconscious gesture of helplessness. "There's nothing you can do for him, Shah."

For perhaps the first time he saw in her face full awareness of her own power. It glowed in her; not a lust, like Amalthea's, but nor was there much modesty in it. It was as if, after protracted evasions, she had finally been confronted with what she was, only to find that she really rather liked it. She was proud of what she could do, with a clear calm pride that was neither arrogant nor shy. She said quietly, "You're wrong. There's nothing you can do. There is something I can do."

Chaucer did not understand her. Paul did. Some resentment but more fear thickened his voice. "No. Shah, I told you –"

"I know: too dangerous to try. But the Drones shared my pain when I was hurt and I'm going to try to share Michal's now."

"You can't share in his death!"

"I don't intend to. But if I can make it easier for him, take some of the hurt and some of the fear, even if I can't begin to recompense him for what we've done to him with our scheming, still maybe it'll mean something to him. Maybe just walking part of the way with him will help. I know there's a risk. I owe it to him to try." She grinned suddenly. "Give me your hand and I'll dare anything."

She stretched her strong hand towards him. Paul wanted her to dare nothing, but he could not refuse her request. Feeling his own impotence like hemlock, bitter in his belly and leaden in his veins, he took her hand; and he held onto it, dropping to his knees to support her limp vacated body, when she slipped inside Michal.

Shah had been a telepath all her life. Most of that time she had used her talent instinctively; only in the comparatively short period that she had known Paul had she received any kind of training. But if her education had been limited her experience was without parallel. From childhood she had tripped in and out of the minds around her, often without any particular reason, using her perception with the same abandon as others use their eyes. She was as familiar with the private thoughts of men and women – whose faces she had long forgotten and whose names she had never known – as her contemporaries had been with their playgrounds: the markets, arcades and plazas of the caravanserai town where she was born. She had wandered, unsuspected, through the mental processes of soldiers, prostitutes, philosophers, thieves, murderers, grocers, barbarians, royalty and a poet. She had ventured, with more difficulty and at some cost to both of them, into the brilliant ice-diamond intellect, sprawling and infinitely complex, where reason warred eternally with rage for the possession of Paul's soul. She had known minds in the passionate heights of love and hatred, in terror and in triumph, going about their trivial human concerns and aspiring to godhood. She had never tasted death. She entered Michal's fading animus without preconception. Even so, she was surprised.

She expected to find him lost, hurt and frightened, spinning out of control in the dark. She did not expect to find him – when she finally found him, deep within the shrinking boundaries of his existence – calm, content, fully aware and happy if somewhat startled to see her.

"Shah! Whatever are you doing here?"

The place where they met was without dimension, either of space or time. There was neither visible light nor patent darkness, and there was no sound. They spoke some other way.

"I was – concerned," stammered Shah. "I – I thought I could help."

She felt him smiling. The smile was not part of his broken body but an expression of his undamaged mind. An existential smile, it hung in nothing, a distillation of the pure essence of a young man with a great if untried capacity for happiness. "Sweet Shah, my dear and idiotic friend! Whatever makes you think I need help? This is the one task even I may be relied upon to complete without error. Some of us need help to be born, many of us require help repeatedly throughout our lives, but the most ineffectual of us can die without assistance."

Shah was stung by his obvious amusement although neither immune to his logic nor unimpressed by his new assurance. "I thought you would be hurting. I was going to share your pain. I suppose you find that pretty laughable, too."

Michal's gentle spirit was immediately contrite. "Forgive me. That was a brave and kindly thought. But quite unnecessary. I have no pain. Pain is the prerogative of the viable. I feel nothing. Go back now. Remember me fondly."

"There is time yet. I want to ask you something."

But the time was limited. The dimensionless place at the hub of Michal's contracting world was subtly changing, stretching thin, becoming remote and rarefied. There was no sense of menace, but Shah was aware that Michal was gravitating away from her, drawn – not pushed – by forces beyond her perception. It was as if

Amalthea's gun had torn a small rent in the fabric of space, allowing the void beyond – call it death, call it paradise, call it entropy – to rush in and claim him; and he was willing enough to be claimed only Shah was there stopping the hole, obstructing the process. "Ask."

"Why, Michal? Was it for me? Was it for Paul? Was it Amalthea you were protecting? Why did you *do* it?"

A kaleidoscope of possibilities flashed before her inward eye. She saw – or something – her own body an awkward, bony tangle, all head and knees, heaped in a corner with important pieces at impossible angles. She saw Paul spread-eagled on the floor, his outflung arms bare to the turned-back cuffs of Michal's capacious shirt, his face destroyed. And she saw Amalthea, imperious as ever, gleaming with silver and malice, surveying her shrunk empire from the eminence of her throne with daunting dead eyes from which the glow had not yet perished. The only death he seemed not to have contemplated was his own.

He said, "I am not sure. I think I just got tired of being pushed around."

Shah felt shame rising through her like a blush. "Oh Michal, I'm sorry."

"Regret nothing. I have no regrets. Nothing in my life was worth one half so much as chancing it for you."

The rent was stretching, the press of the void growing more insistent. The fibres of Michal's mind were aligning to it like iron-filings to a magnet. He was ready, even eager, to obey its summons, his attention straining towards it like a dog on a leash. Shah was aware that she was holding him back but could not bring herself to give him up. She could not relinquish something which she valued and could not have again.

"Shah, you must leave now," urged Michal.

"I don't want to." Even to herself her voice – voice? – sounded petulant, like a child sent early to bed.

"You must. I have to go. You know that. For your own safety –"

It was too late. The rent ripped wide with the scream of calico.

Entropy poured in, instantly everywhere. In the madly rushing nothing Shah lost Michal, lost herself – was swept away, helpless as a matchstick on an ocean swell, without direction or perception or any control of the situation, not knowing which way up she was or where she was going, or even, with any certainty, who she was any more. Her senses fled; comprehension, identity fled; fear – not hysterical but desolate, soul-deep – flooded into the vacuum. Too dangerous to try, Paul had said, but she had known better; had to know better, be stronger, be cleverer, and now she faced dissolution in the vortex of her own pride. She felt herself stretching in the tow of unknowable forces. She knew herself lost.

She heard – heard? – her name. The familiar shape of the word pulsed through the chaos of Michal's collapsing synapses like a beacon. Far and faint and somehow fragile as it was, it gave direction to her wilderness, something to focus on and struggle towards, and in struggling she felt herself grow stronger and the voice grow nearer and the chaos wear thinner until only a fine membrane, a kind of surface tension, separated her from freedom and substance. She raked at the membrane with mental claws and the energy of desperation, and the world came back.

She found herself cradled with infinite care in the arms of a man she hardly knew, gazing into the rosy bearded face and the concerned gem-bright eyes of the Chancellor of the Hive of Mithras. When he saw intelligence in her look Chaucer smiled gravely for a moment; only a moment, then the smile faded and he set her gently down on the dais by Amalthea's throne. He turned away from her.

"She is all right, Paul. What about you?"

Something between a grunt and a groan was his reply. Paul was hunched against the wall by Michal's dead body, bent over his bent knees, clutching his head in his hands as if it might otherwise fall and roll away. Chaucer could not see his face, but the knuckles of his hands were white and their heels ground into his temples.

"Paul. Can I help?"

"No. Leave me alone." His voice was pinched, breathy with effort.

"At least let me –"

"Don't touch me."

Chaucer straightened up, chewing his lip. His searching eye settled on the flask on Amalthea's table. The Hive brewed a characteristically vicious liqueur from beans, but the Empress had never indulged; fortunately, on Mithras even the spring-water had teeth. He filled a goblet with it.

As he passed her Shah caught his arm. "What happened, please?"

Chaucer shook his head. His disturbed eyes held her briefly and then slid away. "I do not know."

"You were here; you saw!"

His eyes came back and gripped her like hard hands. "I do not understand what I saw. I do not know what happened. I do not want to talk about it." He shrugged off her hand and went to Paul.

Kneeling, he gently pushed Paul's clenched hands down and, supporting his head as a woman might a child's, raised the goblet to his lips. "Drink it, you crazy obstinate inhuman son of a star-djinn," he murmured tenderly.

Before they left the high cell Paul went to Amalthea and took the stolen key from her throat. Then he wrung the two jewels off her dead hand. Chaucer raised his leonine head, and his sea-grey eyes flared angrily.

Paul favoured him with a wan smile. "You think we're just going to walk out of here? They aren't deaf, down below. They know something's been going on up here, and when we try to leave they'll want to know what. I don't want to have to fight my way through them today."

Chaucer's eyebrows climbed. "Today?"

Paul rocked a hand. "Tomorrow either, for preference. These'll get us through. You people have spent too long backing away off from these rings to stand up to them now. They'll wonder what it means, they'll watch us like hawks, and the minute we're out of the door they'll be up here like greased lightning, but Shah wearing these stones will see us safely through a mob that neither your authority or my martial expertise would make much impression on." He tossed the rings to Shah who put them on.

Chaucer nodded slowly. His gaze took in the still commanding sliver of moonlight on the black throne. "You could just be right."

"I have to be."

With respect finally established as the currency, Chaucer felt free to dislike the mercenary a little. "Are you always this sure of yourself?"

"I have to be."

Shah walked down the levels of the Hive, her head held high, green and claret fires dancing on her hand, the men at her shoulders. The Hive people lined every corridor, clustered around every stair. Like children witnessing something momentous, those at the front hanging back and those behind pressing forward, with fearful and sullen faces, they seemed an endless arcade of living statues, only the hoarse whisper of their breath like a tide over shingle breaking the clamouring hush. Their avid eyes clutched at her passing, hung upon her step, drank in the jewels. The anarchy of their racing minds jostled her brain. She looked to neither side, concentrating all her attention on keeping a steady pace and a firm course through the crowding dregs of Amalthea's empire.

Only once, anticipating the challenge that would explode the illusion of sanctity and bring the Hive down about their heads, did she invoke the power of her perception in their defence. Balrig staggered back, palms clapped to his ears, a ringing of confusion in his brain and no lingering recollection why his mouth was open. He closed it and sat down on a step to nurse his head, and the two aliens and the strange-eyed Chancellor passed unchallenged and so gained the safety of the tall door.

Shah passed through the high portal and down the steps and set out across the clearing towards the distant shiny shuttle without breaking her stride. But Paul paused halfway down the steps and looked back. Chaucer had stopped in the doorway, a sea of faces crowding at his back. "Aren't you coming with us?"

Chaucer made a helpless gesture with his arms. "How can I leave them now?"

"It's the only way you'll get them off Mithras before the situation here hits the fan."

"I know. Unless –"

Paul squinted up at him suspiciously. "Unless what?"

"Unless you hire us a ship and send it here. I could hold them together until it arrived."

"Hell's teeth, Chaucer," snarled Paul, "you think I've nothing better to do than run round the galaxy after you people? Why stop at hiring it, maybe you'd like me to fly it too, and then give you a hand loading the furniture? I've got a living to make, you know?"

"I know."

"It's not as if I owed you anything."

"I know."

"I mean, it's been interesting, but I don't leave here with any sense of being eternally in your debt. I feel no crushing compulsion to grovel, suck and crawl my way into your affections for old times' sake. My sentimental attachment to the Hive has worn thin to the point of through. I can ride my burners out of here without a backward look, and if years and light-years hence I casually hear that something weird happened on Mithras and there aren't any people there any more, the only worry I'm going to have is remembering where I heard that name before. You understand? I don't need your problems."

"I understand." There was a smile in the Chacellor's voice. When Paul stopped throwing angry looks around him he saw a smile in his eyes, and it was clear that only considerable physical command kept a smile from his lips.

Paul scowled at him. He scowled at the men clustered behind him, who did not know what they were hearing but were somehow aware of its significance. He turned away and scowled after Shah's receding figure. Then he turned back. "It'll cost you."

"Same fee?"

"Same fee. *And* the cost of hiring the transporter. And I'll take it with me. I wouldn't ask anyone to trust you lot."

Shah walked out to the waiting shuttle alone, glad of the quiet, glad of the chance to think. Her mind was in a peculiar state of frozen turmoil, like a basket of snakes with the lid firmly clamped on. There was a great stillness about her and in her, but in her innermost self of all she knew it was spurious, a façade of calm disguising the seething ferment in her brain. She desperately needed a chance to get what had happened at the top of the Hive straight in her mind. She thought she knew what had happened after Michal died, she believed in the miracle, and she was afraid to approximately equal degrees of the consequences of being right and the disappointment of being wrong.

Preoccupied as she was, it was some moments before she became aware of the small grey figure silently watching from the margin of the forest. It was Surgeon. Shah inclined her head in recognition, but at first made no move towards him: she was considerably uncertain as to the current state of relations between herself and Mithras. But Surgeon neither approached nor made to leave, and at length curiosity overcame caution. Groping ahead with her perception, using it as a blind man's cane to forewarn of hazard, she walked across the bare earth to meet him.

"You won, then," said Surgeon.

"Did we? It doesn't feel much like a victory."

"The boy died."

"Yes." She felt her scalp crawl. "How did you know?"

"We are Mithras."

Slow appreciation of what the enigmatic answer implied crept over like the shadow of an eclipse. She was again smitten by the sense of overwhelming power which cloaked the Drones in their own land, an aura almost of majesty which made a strange but not absurd contrast with their homely appearance. "He's with – He is –?" She did not know the words to express the concept of incorporation.

"Is he less of Mithras than we?"

Shah looked towards the Hive. A solitary figure detached itself from the background and moved out into the open. It would be Paul; even at that distance she sensed the weariness which enveloped him like a shroud, not a weakness but a flatness, a loss of elasticity. He walked like an automaton.

Surgeon's gaze had followed hers. His attitude remained equivocal.

"You freed him."

"I had to. He is my friend. I couldn't let you kill him."

"No?"

"What he did, that hurt you – it wasn't how it seemed. He didn't blast the forest for Amalthea. He didn't know there were people there. There was no way he could know about you, about Mithras."

"We cannot forgive, you know. But we do understand that."

"We're leaving now. In a few months a ship will come to evacuate the Hive people. Your planet will be your own again."

"We never gave it up."

Shah nodded and smiled and began to turn away. Then she thought of something. She fumbled at her hand. "You'd better have these back." She proffered a palm of ruby and emerald fire.

The Drone touched her hand, closing it. "Keep them. To remember us by."

"You think I might forget?" Her face went serious. "I shan't forget my promise, either. I'll be your balladeer."

Surgeon's far-sighted, berry-brown eyes roved the green fields and settled on the small, lonely figure of the trudging man. "He was strong."

"He will be strong again."

The forest dweller glanced at her and something that was almost an expression ghosted across his leathery face. Then he turned and in three stumpy strides vanished into the thicket.

Shah's great eyes flew wide with a last wild notion and she shouted after him, "What about Amalthea?"

An answer reached her from nowhere. "And is not Amalthea more of Mithras than most of us?"

When Paul came they went up to "Gyr" almost in silence; not the familiar unstrained silence of easy companionship but a tenser quiet, terse with the recognition that a thing had happened between them that rocked the very foundations on which their shared life was built. It made them as strangers. Once, dull with fatigue, Paul made an awkward and unconvincing essay at conversation and almost broke Shah's heart.

He spent half an hour bringing "Gyr's" computers up to date while Shah hovered in the background, watching covertly, aching for communication and fearing rebuttal as she had not since the first days of their acquaintance. She was still wavering when he finished and straightened up, stretching cautiously. Then he walked off the flight-deck, passing her without a word or a glance.

"Paul!"

The look he gave her was furtive, fugitive. "I can't do any more today. We can leave first thing tomorrow. I have to get some sleep."

She could not argue with that. "Yes. All right." He went on through the hatch. Shah stayed alone on the flight-deck for some minutes, feeling the silence along her skin like cool air, wanting to fight it but not knowing where to aim her blows. Finally she admitted defeat and went to her own cabin.

She got as far as taking off her jacket and shoes. Then, sitting morosely on the edge of her bunk with one shoe in her hand, she experienced a sudden access of indignation. She shot to her feet, slammed out of her cabin and stalked down the companionway to Paul's, determination stiffening the fibres of her being like starch. She threw open the door. "Listen, you –"

Paul was hunched over the chart-table in his cabin, his back to the hatch, his shoulders slumped. He did not turn at the drama of her entrance.

Impatience immediately gave way to concern. "Paul? What's the matter?"

His head hung. His voice was thick and querulous. "I can't get this bloody shirt off." He sounded close to tears.

Blood seeping from his wounds had crusted the fabric to his skin. Shah soaked it off with a warm sponge. Then she made some coffee and brought it in "Apathy" and "Celibacy". They sat cross-legged at opposite ends of Paul's bunk, facing each other. Paul buried his face in his mug.

Sipping at her own, watching from under her fringe, Shah said, "I have to know what happened."

His eyes flicked up and down, hunted. "You know what happened. Michal died. In spite of your intervention, he still died."

"Yes. Did I?"

She saw him shudder. He did not reply.

"I went into Michal's mind because I thought I could help him," she said carefully, picking her words, working at staying calm. "I found he needed no help, but before I could leave his death broke through and enveloped both of us. I was lost. I lost Michal, lost my way. I thought I was dying. Did I die?"

Paul would not meet her gaze. He looked everywhere else, with a dismally shallow pretence of idleness. "Patently not."

"As you will. Then someone called me by my name. You."

"That's right."

"From inside. You followed me inside. Didn't you?"

He could not cope with her interrogation. He knew what she was driving at. Whatever he had done in the Hive room, it had left his brain pulsing with pain and possibilities. The pain was quiescent now but the other was eating him up, like fever. The last thing he needed was a cross-examination. Tired as he was, he started to his feet and made for the door. But he did not leave. He had never run from his enemies, felt suddenly ashamed of fleeing from Shah. He slowly turned. His face was twisted. Shah's gut twisted up in sympathy.

He leaned back against the door, his palms braced flat against its cool plane. The words came hard. "I don't know what happened. When the boy was dead and you were still in there – I tried to reach you. I knew I couldn't, but I tried. And then my head –" Mere memory was enough to make him flinch. "All the same, I know what didn't happen and so do you. I'm not a telepath, Shah, I no longer have any extra-sensory capacity. That part of my brain was burned out with a laser. Whatever happened, it had to be your faculties at work. I have none."

Shah did not believe it. Starling-coloured highlights danced down the length of her straight dark hair as she firmly shook her head. "No. The power was outside me. I had nothing, was nothing, then. If I was not dead I would have died, but that somehow you came for me and did something that hurt your head and saved my life. Those are the facts. We may interpret them as we will."

"What do you think – that I'm lying to you?" He was trying to whistle up enough anger to cover the hollow fear in his eyes. "That all the time I've known you I've been carefully hiding, for reasons of my own, a full range of extra-sensory abilities from mind-reading to teleportation? That I pretended to be taken in by Amalthea's lies for the sheer pleasure of being shot, carved up and generally abused by the Hive people, and that in order to protect the illusion I manifested a detailed and – if I say it myself – persuasive impression of a man bleeding to death in a cactus garden? Is that what you think?"

"Of course not. Oh Paul, do sit down, you look terrible."

"Maybe that's part of the illusion too," he said snidely. But he came back glowering and sat beside her on the bunk.

"I never for a moment believed you'd lied to me," said Shah. "But now something remarkable has happened, and it occurs to me to wonder if perhaps they lied to you."

His eyes burned her. The hope he had fought against had gained a foothold. That and the fear fed on each other, making him a battlefield. "Explain."

She took a deep breath and tried. "The people who – made – you went to a lot of trouble to get a telepath. They bred you, from God knows what stock, for the inherent trait and then they engineered, manipulated and trained you until they had refined a supreme and, to the best of their knowledge, unique talent. If they'd known about me perhaps they wouldn't have bothered, but that's neither here nor there. But you were more than they bargained for. Your powers and personality were too much for them to control. You frightened the life out of them, and finally they felt they had no choice but to – incapacitate you. To protect themselves."

Paul said in his teeth, "They crippled me. They used a laser to burn every vestige of perception out of my head."

"But did they? They wouldn't do it lightly, not after all their work. They would think very hard and consider all the alternatives. You were very young: it must have occurred to them that as you grew up you might become more amenable. If there was any chance, they'd want to preserve the option."

She felt the tension of his body where his shoulder touched hers. "What are you suggesting?"

"I'm not suggesting anything, I don't know enough to. But what I'm wondering is this. Suppose they didn't burn it out – that was only what they told you. Suppose what they actually did was isolate it, wall off that part of your brain – behind a barrier of scar tissue or somesuch. Would you know the difference?"

"I don't know." He was trembling now. "You've been in there – what do you think?"

"Paul, I wouldn't begin to know. Your mind is like nowhere I've ever been anyway. But it's possible, isn't it?"

"Dear God," he whispered, "it's possible."

"And not knowing it was there still," Shah hurried on, "you've managed without it all these years. But today, for me, you tried beyond any human expectation of trying. You nearly killed yourself trying. What if all that effort broke down a portion of the barrier and let your perception out? Just for a moment, just long enough for you to reach me. What then, Paul? What then?"

"I don't know." He touched his fingertips to his aching skull with reverence and wonder. "I don't know."

Shah put her arm around him and lowered her head onto his shoulder. "Me neither. But Paul, I think we should try to find someone who does."

They remained like that, quiet and unmoving, for a long time. The ship slept about them, only murmuring peacefully to itself as systems that were designed to tackle the distances between stars drowsed their way through one 85-minute orbit after another. Below, the languid turning of Mithras brought slow night on the Hive.

Paul thought that Shah too was sleeping, and was considering how he might put her to bed without waking her, but she was not asleep. She moved her head on his shoulder languorously, rubbing against his neck like a cat.

"I wonder how Michal likes being a planet," she yawned.